Big Bend

Winner of the Flannery O'Connor Award for Short Fiction

Big Bend

STORIES BY BILL ROORBACH

The University of Georgia Press › *Athens & London*

Paperback edition published in 2014 by
The University of Georgia Press
Athens, Georgia 30602
www.ugapress.org

Designed by Erin Kirk New
Set in 10 on 14 Berkeley Oldstyle Medium

Most University of Georgia Press titles are
available from popular e-book vendors.

Printed digitally

The Library of Congress has cataloged the
hardcover edition of this book as follows:

Roorbach, Bill.
Big Bend : stories / by Bill Roorbach.
174 p. ; 21 cm.
Contents: Thanksgiving—Blues machine—A job at
Little Henry's—Taughannock Falls—Fredonia—Lone-
liness—Fog—Anthropology—Big Bend.
ISBN 0-8203-2283-0 (alk. paper)
    1. United States—Social life and customs—20th
century—Fiction. I. Title
PS3568.O6345 B54 2001
813'.54—dc21   00-044729

Paperback ISBN 978-0-8203-4723-3

British Library Cataloging-in-Publication Data available

For Kurt Carlson, for Jon Zeeman, and, as always, for Juliet Karelsen

CONTENTS

Big Bend

Thanksgiving

When the phone rings in the empty loft Ted knows exactly who it is: exquisite Mary, gentle Mary, tough Mary and brainy—his brother's wife—for whom Ted would fall in a minute if such things were permitted. She seems cold as they climb through some small talk, gets to the point fast, warms to her task: "Oh Teddy, really, you have to come this year. You ought to come this year. Lily wants to show you her watercolors." Lily is the oldest of Ernest and Mary's three little daughters. "And your mom would like you here."

"Why doesn't this Mom person call me herself?" Ted says, growing testy despite his resolution: this year at Thanksgiving he's going to be part of the family again, no explosions, no tumult, no bubbling in the bosom. He knows where Mary's calling from, hears Elrod's raspy barking, hears the TV in his parents' sumptuous den (where doubtless his mother is standing focused like a laser on Mary and the phone).

Mary eats a laugh. "Well, she's right here."

"No fooling." Teddy sees it perfectly: Mary grinning, handing the phone to Mom against feeble protests, Mom's hands up to keep this difficulty away, Mary smiling more forcedly and holding the receiver against Mom's ear.

Too late; the old gal has to speak: "Well. Teddy. When are we coming?"

"I don't know, Mother. Wednesday? Thursday morning? I've got a ton of work: a lady on Beekman Place wants a portrait, and I'm showing slides at two galleries."

From his mother, silence.

Ted says, "And the Met, well not the Met exactly, but this very consequential curatorial entity wants to . . ."

"Well, marvelous. Whenever you get here is exactly right."

Now Lily has the phone, no good-bye from Mom. "Uncle Teddy?"

"Hi, Lily Loops. Halloo. Are you coming for Thankspiglet?"

"Oh, Uncle Teddy!"

As always his niece's giggle is the most perfect music Ted has ever heard. She likes a sense of conspiracy so he whispers: "Bring the turkey in a paper bag. Bring eleven cranberries."

"Uncle Teddy, come on!" Oh, her laughter, this laughter right now, this is the most beautiful thing Ted has ever made. The kids! For the kids he won't be off his rocker anymore.

⟩ ⟩ ⟩

There's not a dime in sight for Ted Lyons. And not a paintbrush either. He hasn't made the trip to a gallery—not even SpaceSpace on Avenue D—with slides in hand in a year or more, hasn't *shot* slides for six months, hasn't produced anything to photograph. *Consequential curatorial entity!* Crap. This pompous spur-of-the-moment phrasing plays over and over in his mind, a rebuke. Back to the nuthouse, Mom must be thinking. His past success as a painter, life before his—ahem—*rest time,* offers no succor for these angry days. He and his supposed art are in some kind of extended eclipse, the needling voices in his head so loud he can't paint in the same room with them.

The lady on Beekman Place wanting a portrait is a fat lie (though once Ted fixed a toilet in someone's brownstone there). His Mr. Fix-it ad in the back of the *Village Voice* ran out in August and he hasn't had enough money to run another. Monte Dorfman, his comfortably rich roommate and true friend, normally good for a loan, is far away—a tour of Asia and Australia—and won't be back for three months.

Ted boils water and makes himself a plate of miserably unadorned Ziti and feels maybe a little of the romance he as a college student might have seen here. He is an artist. He is surely going mad, and for the second time. He will not ask for help, however, will not give a clue to anyone. If he does, it's back to you-know-where. And with you-know-who paying for it. And finally, the last brick in the wall of romance: Teddy is in danger of starving. Or at least of being hungry: there're two or three nights of eating in that big ShopRite Ziti box.

Midnight, he empties Monte's change jar, which has enough nickels and dimes for two beers at Milady's, corner of Thompson and Prince, where two beers bought gets you one on Frankie, who will knock the bar and say, "This one's with me, pal." And knock the bar all night with a kind eye on the pile of pennies Ted scoots around in front of him, barely shiny with nickels.

A few beers, a half dozen, that changes the complexion of things.

❭ ❭ ❭

There's no getting back to sleep. Teddy thinks of Thanksgiving dinner and Lily Loops and Beaner and his sister Kelly and beautiful Mary and Mom. And Dollar Dad and Big Brother Ernest and Little Bro Jim. It's the family that's going to save him. Going to have to. He thinks of Monte and Jennifer in Southeast Asia and Professor Mtuboto at Brown University and the one painting no one ever had any doubt about, Ted's thesis work, "Self Portrait with Attitude," an enormous picture in oils of himself with ten feet of blank canvas to one side: his first masterpiece (that is, the first real piece of himself to reach canvas), already ten years old, moldering in some generous lady's collection. For the two thousand bucks (his first fortune) Ted wishes he still had the painting, wishes maybe he'd never bought the hope the money had afforded him. Because in a complicated web he once had a handle on, that sale launched the events that took him to Riverview Heights (formerly known as Riverview Sanitarium), a lovely place with a campus like a college and doctors like calm parents.

Four A.M. and he's not sleepy at all, still ruminating furiously, still entertaining the comments of all the observers of his ruminations, a clear idea having entered his head: the possibility of his own change. He could get a job like Ernest's, wed a woman like Mary, live in a suburb like Newcastle, Connecticut, his own hometown, work his way toward respectability and honor, explore the possibilities of commercial art (his dad's perennial suggestion), stop thinking of commercial art as selling out (Monte's phrase, Monte in Cambodia) but as *buying in*, as *getting real* (as younger brother Jimmy would say). Because a woman like Mary you interested only with success, with brains, with self-love and self-power like Ernest's. Madness was out.

Ted rose and began searching cushions of the bad furniture in his loft—Monte's loft, if you thought in terms of leases and rent and who had his shit together. Three shineless quarters in the yellow vinyl chair, a dime in the heater, nineteen cents in the cracks of the warped old floor. Sixteen one-dollar bills in Monte's desk drawer. Smiling gods of heaven!

Meds or Jack Daniel's?

⟩ ⟩ ⟩

On the eve of Thanksgiving Teddy rolls out an entire bolt of the Canson Mi-Teintes paper his father bought him those two hopeful years ago. Dad kindly put out some mean cash at Pearl Paints down on Canal Street: "You got to spend money to make money," misunderstanding the whole artist game with unusual heart. Fifty feet of the thick, beautiful paper, forty-five inches high, and Teddy gets to work on his idea for Thanksgiving, his idea for what he can add to the festivities and still have enough cash to pay for the train ride home. It's a mural with serious sections and comic sections, a Thanksgiving card, a love poem to his family, his thanks for their forbearance. He sips Jack Daniel's and puts his nieces in there: Lily Loops and the Bean as tidy little Pilgrims; the babies, April and Erin, as cherubs on the back of spotted fawns. He paints his tall mother slightly unhappy as the Pilgrim matriarch, cigarette in hand, paints Dad beside her in a kind of Pilgrim three-piece suit with musket and briefcase. He paints quickly, a succession of photographs in hand, quickly and with a humor that comes of using up the last of a formerly huge supply of paint, a supply that once seemed like hope itself. Good brushes, too, worn but well cared for. Teddy shows his brawny young sister Kelly beneath an enormous and laden picnic table, holding the whole thing up with one hand and wearing a Grecian tunic—a lady Hercules. He captures perfectly his brother Jimmy and Jimmy's wife, Connie, in jogging outfits, their new twin Volvos tethered to teamed horses. He gets Elrod in there and a good deal of Edenic garden, both to honor his mom. He paints Ernest lolling magisterially in a cloud, a stern but beneficent god blowing fortune from on high. He's painting hard, he's painting fast, he's in a lather, he's damn good, he's got whiskey in his blood. "The mural is really working," say the onlookers. "It's a pageant!" He plays with the long composition, repeating figures: there's Dad off to work; there's Kelly slaying buffalo; there's Lily and April *sur l'herbe* in their swim-team suits, lunching with the painter; there's Jimmy flinging U.S. currency to the wind; there's Connie dandling Erin; there's Ernest intently making a drawing, his first.

Later Ted realizes he's put Mary in the only Native American costume, painted her at both ends of the absurdly elongated table. At one end she gazes approvingly at the Ted figure having his *Dejeuner*; at the other she holds the hand of another Ted figure, the two of them looking up, oh, looking up and pointing at Ernest, the great pale god , unbearably handsome.

They will like this poster. They will! The whole family, and then Teddy can ask them for succor.

⟩ ⟩ ⟩

At the Newcastle Train Station Thanksgiving morning Ted steps down into the bright sun, sees a row of twelve-hour parking meters, a gas station, a bent Lions Club sign, the drive-up window of the First Newcastle Bank, a particular tree, all of it fraught with sad memories: Marianne Oplennoff for one, Dad in his business suit for another, the daily commute.

No time to get misty: Dad rockets into the station parking lot in his new Humvee, skids in the gravel, stops so the passenger door is exactly at Ted's hand, leans hard (no seat belt), flings the door open, shouts, "Son, get in."

Lily's in the back seat, grinning. She's a small version of Mary, her hair long and black, gap between her big front teeth, flannel shirt twenty sizes too big. Ted pokes his bulkily rolled mural into the back beside her, throws Monte's daypack on top of her, just for fun.

"Lillian," he says deeply, knowing she'll laugh. And she does, and puts a long little hand on his shoulder as he gets in, pats him expressively, pure love and acceptance, holds the daypack in her lap.

Ted pats her hand back and pat pat pat it's a joke. On impulse then he leans awkwardly to hug Dad and worse, kisses Dad on his stubbled cheek. Dad is embarrassed, so hits the gas, throwing gravel, and they're off, just one mile to the old home.

The enormous vehicle has the old-home smell—Dad's cigarettes, probably, and his shoe polish—and it gives Ted the old-home feeling, a mixture of comfort and dread, with the difference that now he actually recognizes that dread's in the mix. Today recognition adds consternation, not comfort. Dad drives very fast, shooting his spindly right arm out in front of Ted at every stop to protect him from his own inertia at stops as if he's a kid again.

In the back seat Lily the Looper studies the inside of the rolled mural. She speaks into it, hollow echo: "Calling Uncle Teddy. Come in, Theodore Lyons. Are you going to stay this time?"

"Not you, too," says Ted.

Dad chortles. "Of course he's going to stay! He'll stay the weekend! We'll have turkey sandwiches!"

"Maybe, Dad. Maybe not. I've got a lot of work, a ton. I've got a job I might do Saturday." There's no job on Saturday. There's no job at all. Ted's head swims: Jack Daniel's hangover. Someone is telling him to get home. This he fights. He'll ask for help. He'll ask Mary, perhaps, and she can ask Mom, who in turn can go to Dad.

Into the tube of the mural Lily intones: "You don't like us."

"Lily Loop Lungfish, you mind your manners!" says Ted, in imitation of an angry Ernest. Lily screams, getting the joke, then laughs and laughs, sniffing through her nose, embarrassed to let it out.

"Mom's got a thirty-pounder!" says Dad.

⟩ ⟩ ⟩

The house is still there, Victorian and tall, pure white everything, surrounded by a neat yard and giant oaks, not a stray leaf in sight, not a stray blade of grass. The fall has been warm so the lawn's still green. The sky is blue, the air is clean, the smells are familiar to the point of memory. The grand over-arched driveway is full of cars, license plates from all over: Ted's siblings. Lily takes his hand and walks him up the driveway, feeling somehow the formality of the situation, seeming to know that it's she who must guide Ted back to the flock.

Jimmy is first out of the house to greet them. He's all smiles, wearing a tie. Ted's heart wells at sight of his little brother, who's not so little; in fact, Jimmy's a big man, over six feet, over two hundred pounds, polished and smart, thick glasses, wet hair. The brothers meet under the portico in an uncomfortable hug. Dad has hung back, thin and stiff and suspicious as an old dog. He turns abruptly and makes for the toolshed where his lawn machines will be.

Jimmy says, "You look like shit," which is a joke.

"He's tired," Lily says protectively.

"Let's go over to the mall in Stamford and get you some clothes tomorrow," Jimmy says.

"I'm fine," says Ted.

Then Connie's at the screen door—Jimmy's wife. "Uncle Ted!" she cries. Lily's little sister Bean peeks around Connie, looks impatiently at Ted, spins and leaves. In the foyer (potted plants, framed photos, a painting by Kelly, two drawings by Lily, nothing by Ted, nothing in the whole house by Ted) the whole gang turns out. Ernest is impassive, holds out his hand for a shake, doesn't quite smile, looks ready to give a speech. Kelly laughs in words—ha ha ha—hugging Ted and kissing his cheek, a mountain of cheer. And there's little April, looking pissed, her fist in her mouth. Beaner makes her way back into the foyer, dragging Mom, who inspects Ted from head to toe. "What a crowd," Mom says, and turns on heel.

"You been eating enough there in New York?" says Jimmy, genuinely concerned.

And Ernest says, "Tofu," derisively, then looks Ted over, sneakers to ponytail, clearly finds him wanting.

"He'll eat today!" Kelly says brightly. She's a sweetie, really a sweetie.

"Ziti, I eat," says Ted, attempting good cheer, but sounding merely cryptic, even to himself. "Tofu's more Monte's speed."

Suddenly there's the smell of turkey, and Ted relaxes, lets Lily tug him into the little parlor off the kitchen, sits himself down, pulls Lily down beside him on the arm of the big chair, three-year-old April eyeing them both skeptically.

Jimmy says, "I'll help Mom," and drifts back to the kitchen. There's a record spinning on the parlor turntable, vague holiday music, a fire in the parlor fireplace even though it's a sauna in here already. One by one the family files in. Lily pats Ted's shoulder. Baby Erin starts to fuss in Connie's arms so everyone looks to her.

"Thanks, Lil," says Ted, seriously, under his breath.

"For what?" says she, also seriously. Connie has heard, looks puzzled. Ernest stalks in and leans on the bookshelf, wiry and small as Dad, resumes his appraisal of Ted, visibly repressing some imperious command to get Lily off the arm of the chair. He says, "Monte and tofu in Greenwich Village," meaning: Doesn't that just say it all!

April does a somersault to much applause.

Kelly laughs—ha ha ha ha ha, says, "Have you found yourself a girl?"

And Ernest says, "Tofu," again.

Irritable Mom in the kitchen yells out, "One hour!" and Jimmy comes flying comically back into the parlor.

Ha ha ha ha ha, barks Kelly.

Then Mary steps in from the kitchen, drying the gravy boat, having rinsed out the dust of a year. "Teddy Lyons," says she.

"Mary Meharg Lyons," says Ted in the same tone, which is appraising and affectionate at once.

She says, "The artist is home."

Ted says, "Yeah," and you'd think he was the world's funniest comedian the way everyone laughs.

"Artist," Ernest says, and roars.

Lily says, "He brought a painting."

"You look good," says Mary. "You look very happy and healthy and handsome." She goes back in the kitchen.

"Dad needs me on his chop saw," Ernest says, meaning that some repair is under way. He says, "Artist," again, not exactly shaking his head, tone modulated so carefully you'd have to guess what he meant. Observation? Derision? Kelly follows him out the door.

Jimmy and Connie linger politely. Connie tries for a conversation: "How's New York? I miss New York."

"Is that where you live?" says little Bean.

"Yes," Lily says, patting Ted's shoulder. "He lives in New York City, where we've never been."

⟩ ⟩ ⟩

Just before the big meal Ted gets Lily and Beaner to help him with the forgotten mural. The little girls close the dining room doors and giggle and whisper, loving a conspiracy. Ted stands on the furniture and Dad's spattered stepladder, carefully taping the paint-stiffened paper around three walls and close up under the high ceiling. The mural just clears the tops of the doors and the hutch and the grandfather clock, which tocks. Bean, who is normally as skeptical as Ernest, is thrilled. She holds her belly and stares at the likeness of her little self in the Pilgrim outfit, amazed.

Lily crosses her arms in front of her and gets formal, proffers a review: "I think Grandpa looks perfect except his hair. His hair is white, Uncle Teddy, it's not gray like that."

Ted suppresses the impulse to argue with her. She's nine, for heaven's sake. Also, she's right.

She purses her lips, turns slowly, taking in the mural, one end to the other. She says, "The food looks so real. And Grandma looks perfect, and Uncle Jimmy."

Teddy can't help it, he stands there beaming. Praise is praise, and he hasn't gotten much for months.

"Daddy looks mean," Bean cries, pointing, suddenly having seen the god Ernest in the clouds.

"Why is Aunt Kelly under the table?" says Lily.

"She's holding it up," says Ted.

"And look at me," Lily says. They do, for a full minute, Ted and two children, necks bent back, arms folded. Lily says, "I look stupid."

"You *are* stupid," Beaner says.

Lily says, "And Erin and April, Uncle Teddy, I don't know. Erin and April are the *worst!*"

"Babies are hard," Ted says.

"They look like little animals," says the Bean.

"And why is my mom in a bathing suit?" Lily points.

Eek. Ted needs Lily's eyes to show him that Mary's Native American costume is tiny, a great show of legs and cleavage and burning dark eyes, that old movie poster of Raquel Welch. It's obvious, awful, pure aggression, but the likeness is terrific. Ted has spent a lot more time on her than on the other portraits, and spent it later in

the night of painting, bombed on that whiskey when he should have
bought monthly meds. He has her face perfect down to the expression of pain and caring, has her long hair shining blue and dark as
midnight, has the dent of her lip, the tilt of her head, the knuckles of her hand. But where did the cleavage come from? The oiled
thighs? He wishes for paints to fix her costume, then in a fit of real
grandiosity decides she'll like it.

To Lily he says, "I need help."

Lily looks at him seriously.

"Come carry things, girls," says Ted's mother.

"April and Lily, come help," calls Mary, as if they are miles away.

Ted takes advantage of the empty dining room to raid the liquor
cabinet. He pours several fingers of Wild Turkey into a large orna-
mental cup from the top shelf of the hutch. He drinks fast, pours
again, stows the bottle back in its cabinet, drinks up, steps cheer-
fully into the kitchen fray, pats Miss Bean on her head.

› › ›

Dad, torn away from his machines, sits at the head of the enormous
old table as always, with Bean at his right hand. Mom sits at the foot.
Elrod the mutt, having roused himself, stations himself underneath,
stiffly, seventeen years old, waiting for scraps.

Ted's mural hovers above, surrounding the family on three sides.
Everyone but Kelly thinks it's in bad taste to have painted Kelly
under the table like that, holding things up—but she's proud of her
strength, her size, kindly says she doesn't mind. Ernest seems to like
his position in the clouds, gazes up at himself approvingly. No one
says a word about Mary's costume, though Mary gives Ted a hard
look. His parents barely look up.

Not another word about the mural. Big-hearted Connie, all manners, leaps into the void, takes it upon herself to offer praise, something the Lyonses just aren't good at. She praises the likenesses,

praises Ted's generosity, praises his palette, praises his ingenuity, praises the perspective, the difficult trick of getting everyone in there, praises and praises him in the silent room.

And in the silence that remains when she's through, Dad says grace. Mom and Kelly start passing food around. Ernest's in the same seat he's always been in, exact center of the fire side of the table, equidistant between Mom and Dad. Mary sits beside him. Jimmy and Connie, as always, sit across, neatly dressed. Ted's next to Mary, Lily beside him. Kelly's across from Ted on the piano bench next to Dean, rocking baby Erin, chatting earnestly with April, who is failing to sit quietly. The plates fill up. Forks clatter. The meal commences.

Mom grows sad, sighs and pokes her food. Unasked, unannounced, Dad gives a technology quiz straight from childhood: "At what temperature does all movement stop?" and instantly the siblings are shouting out answers, childlike in competition. Mary and Connie laugh, watching the familiar regression. "Absolute zero," shouts Ernest for the eighth time.

Dad pretends not to hear, won't give Ernest credit, moves on. He says, "By what process is plastic derived from oil?" Jimmy and Ernest and Ted all start talking, none giving ground, none exactly knowing the answer, so, soon and also at once, they shout out jokes to cover themselves, they shout with laughter.

"I paid for how much college?" Dad says.

"Teddy smells like booze," cries Lily.

"Lily smells like baby powder," says Ted. He feels inordinately and absurdly proud that she has chosen to sit beside him, that he is her relative. He tickles her between bites, steals food from her plate.

"You are crazy," she says, patting his shoulder.

"Crazy," Ted says back.

Kelly says, "Oil is turned into plastic by fouling beaches and destroying indigenous populations and by widening the gap between rich and poor and otherwise assuring the hasty end of human culture as we know it and shortly thereafter the death of the earth. Ha ha."

Gentle Connie sees the gauntlet hitting the parched earth, says, "At my office there's this gal who has this dream to fly in a balloon. Of course we just laughed and laughed at her . . ." And keeps trying, though only Mary even pretends to listen.

"Bhopal," Ernest says, cryptically.

". . . signs up for this balloon *tour*."

"For or against?" says Kelly. Ha ha ha.

"Human error," says Dad. "Those Continental Indians are *ineducable*."

"No more quizzes," Mom says.

Connie never gives up, tells the entire story of an eleven-balloon pilgrimage to Cumberland Island, even as Ernest and Dad and Kelly face off three ways about the responsibility of multinational corporations to world culture, not the slightest agreement between them in any direction.

"You want to stop driving your car?" Dad shouts finally, his grin a rictus. "You want Ted to stop using his paint?"

Ted raises his eyebrows.

"Teddy needs help," Lily cries.

"So I guess the lesson is: pursue your dreams," Connie says, and goes silent.

"Maybe we should take the billboard *down*," says Ernest. He means Ted's mural and says it like it's Ted's mural that has caused the ruckus.

"Oh, Ernest," says Mary.

Ted feels himself stiffen.

"Pinkos," says Dad. It's supposed to be a joke but it isn't funny and not even Connie laughs.

"You hurt Ted's feelings," says Lily, soulfully, aggrievedly to her father. She pats Ted's shoulder, says, "You say sorry."

No one is going to say sorry. Everyone turns to eating. The food is gorgeous, delectable, but only Connie says so, a grand "Yum" in the silence: turkey and creamed onions and mashed turnips and sweet potatoes, peas and cranberry chutney and green beans, salad and rolls, lots of rolls.

Ted eats. He wants to tell Lily he is not hurt by Ernest. He wants to tell Lily he's impervious, always was. He wants to tell Lily how he loves her and how funny he thinks she is. He wants to say, Lily, don't worry about me, but he can't because Lily's right, he can't because Lily's seen through him and she's just a kid and she knows about Ted and his pain before Ted even knows. The mural prowls above them. Ted eats with total absorption and the pleasure of it is the most pleasure of any kind he's felt in many weeks, many months, more pleasure than in two years, certainly. One must *ask* for help, as Dr. Teach, his psychiatrist, often says.

The little girls start a song about bluebirds, and everyone just continues to eat in blind concentration, passing bowls around, filling plates, clanking, slurping, sighing.

Mary sits between Ernest and Ted, eating politely, as if she's alone at some diner. Her new red dress is open at the neck, her bra shows ruffles, her cleavage is pale, almost blue. Among the hundred-thousand glossy black hairs on her head there are a hundred strands of gray, which Ted finds stirring, poignant, perfect. He takes a bite of his food, gazes at Mary, gazes away, bites his food, gets lost in his plate. Help, he thinks.

Dad is first to finish, throws his hands up—Touchdown!—smiles broadly, proud of his speed. Ted almost hears him say what Ted wants to hear him say—how good the food is, or how full the fatherly stomach is, or how there's still a little room for pie—but Dad says, "I'd say round up these environmental weenies and pop 'em in a gas chamber somewhere."

Connie laughs absently. Jimmy looks at her, aghast: Connie is Jewish, as Dad well knows. Kelly sighs dramatically, but keeps eating big gulps, has hardly dented the enormous mound of food on her plate.

"Everybody?" says Ted in a rush.

"Don't even say it," says Ernest.

Mary closes her eyes.

Long pause. "I was just going to say that we need to think what the world will be like for these little girls." He smiles benignly, looks at serious Lily, flips a calm open palm toward April, but his heart pounds as if he's being chased, or as if he's been in a crash.

"Can we take the billboard down?" says Ernest, smiling hard. He's still talking about Ted's mural, trying to make it a joke, trying to break the tension, but there's not a jot of humor in his face.

"What I want to know," says Mary evenly, "is the source of all this emotion today."

"Pinkos," says Dad, smiling hard like Ernest, as red in the face.

"Why is everyone fighting?" says April.

"No one's fighting, dear," says Dad.

"Nazis," Kelly says.

Jimmy says: "What's the biggest flounder ever caught?"

Ah, Jimmy. Dad leaps up and rushes to the living room to get the record book and an encyclopedia, and soon he's reading loudly about flatfish, fluke, and flounder.

Suddenly Kelly looks up, fixes Ted in her thoughtful gaze. "If you ask me," she says, "I think it's remarkable how these good upright men can do the work they do for Dow and Union Carbide and still want to *have* children. Jail's too good for them."

"Three hundred forty pounds!" Dad cries.

"No flounder's that big," Ernest says.

"Men and their *stupidity*." This is Mom, just a whisper, barely even a sound, but everyone has heard her. Ted looks at her a minute. She is looking at her plate.

"Have the bulbs gone in?" Kelly says. "Mom Lyons? Have you got the tulips in yet?"

"I've given up on flowers," Mom says.

"Criminey," says Dad.

That's good for more silence.

Ted realizes he's panting, has run a race, is still sprinting. He can't imagine how much whiskey it would take to calm him. He looks to Mary, Mary dressed more formally than the rest of the family, Mary detached in her pleasant way from all the hubbub, an only child who's found herself in the center ring of a circus. Ernest's beautiful Mary. Ted bumps her knee with his own. He looks up at his image of her in the mural. It's sexy, it's good, it's dangerous. He leans to her, whispers, "I love you."

She turns to him, incredulous, and though she's heard him she whispers back, "What?"

And Ted rises, as if to make a toast. He grips the table edge and begins to shake it. Kelly laughs, Ha ha ha, and Lily pats his back. Dad frowns at the rattling of the glassware. Mom says, "Theodore, stop." Ernest shakes his head, rolls his eyes. Jimmy puts his hands up, a calming gesture, looks as though he's seeing a dangerous stranger. Connie laughs at the joke of it, generous as always, keeps laughing even as her face registers that there's no joke.

Ted says, "Everybody?" and shakes the table harder.

"Teddy?" Mary says gently.

"Now, Ted. Ted E. Boy," Dad says soothingly.

Ernest stands too, puts a hand on the table to steady it.

Ted looks up at his mural, the images of each of his siblings, his parents, his nieces, his sisters-in-law. He feels calm, composed, sure of himself for the first time maybe ever. He gives a croak and heaves his side of the table into the air. Ernest's hand upon it is as nothing to Ted's strange strength. The plates across the way slide into Connie's lap, into Jimmy's. Jimmy leaps up, catches the lighted candles as they head for the floor. Bean hops and perches out of the way on her chair, delighted. Big Kelly saves baby Erin, stands and spins, but Connie's too late, stays in her armless chair, catches the table in her lap, shrieks.

Ted heaves again, and the half-carved turkey shoots full speed onto Jimmy's feet before he can put the candles down, before he can do anything. The creamed onions go to Connie, who's squawking, trapped, legs bruised for certain. The yams go to Beaner who— thrilled—knocks her chair over making the catch. The silverware clangs hitting the plates and glasses, which smash in quick series as they hit the hardwood floor. Beaner saves the salad, heavy wooden bowl, holds it a moment, then takes the opportunity to fling lettuce and tomato and round slices of carrot gaily in the air. The center- piece, a bowl of ceramic fruit, slides quickly and crashes. The table- cloth slides away. Baby Erin laughs, Kelly pants, April wails. Only Mary has managed to save her plate, and holds it stoically as Connie in her struggles tilts her own chair till it falls, bringing the huge table all the way down on top of her. Jimmy cries out, gives the table another heave to free his wife. Dad stands with his eyebrows raised, still holding the encyclopedia. Mom moans. Thanksgiving dinner is on the floor. Everyone turns to stare at Ted, stands frozen, mouths open, hands upraised, frozen like that forever.

"Everybody?" Ted says finally. He looks mystified.

"Gonna deck you," says Ernest.

Connie has started to cry.

Lily, she just pats her Uncle Teddy's back.

"We'll get this picked up in no time," Dad says, as if the whole thing were a common Thanksgiving mishap. "No time at all!"

Blues Machine

Rockin' Joe Heath stumbled into the stairwell in nothing but a black Zildjian T-shirt, shushing himself, trying to see right, pounding head. He recalled the old lily pattern of the wallpaper and something about the tattered edges of the carpet over the stairs, but he couldn't remember any act of climbing those stairs or what must have ensued. Connie was dead asleep, a good damn thing. Joe gently closed her door, crept down the hall, tried the next door, sure he'd see tile and toilet, but no, it was stuffed animals and a rumpled single bed.

Oh, Christ, her kids, and Joe with no pants.

Quick. End of the hall, creaking floor, top of the stairs, two more doors, the first a closet (empty shelves except for unmatched washcloths, neatly folded), the next, yes, good, the bath. Mermaid shower curtain. Smell of soap and kid piss. He tripped in, shut the door, addressed the toilet gratefully, yanked a handful of pink toilet paper when he was done, wiped the seat, perfect gentleman. But the toilet would not flush. Rockin' Joe wriggled the handle and rattled it, but the water wasn't going to come.

Medicine cabinet. Squeal of hinges. Plenty prescriptions. One box hair color, "Confident Blonde." Midol. Ointments, pads, puffs, lipsticks, toothbrushes, Q-tips, every stinking thing but aspirin. So

Midol, and close the small door quick as the other shit fell out, long mess of his own blackened hair in the mirror, and his new-trimmed beard, salt and pepper and rocks and mud, Joe tall, mirror low, so nothing of himself above the nose, good thing—didn't want to look in those eyes. He smiled through his mustache to see his pretty teeth (Connie said).

Four Midol in the mouth, down the hatch, but the sink was out, no water. He gagged on the pills, pushed past the door, bounded down the stairs, Midol stuck. Big foyer, old farmhouse, huge living room (bare), dining room (long, elegant, heirloom table), kitchen.

Sink. No stinking water. Joe coughed, the bitter taste of the pills filling his throat and his mouth and his nose. He hopped to the round old refrigerator, whipped the door open slam into the rustic side-board, rattle of jars, plastic pitcher full of pink stuff, Kool-Aid, drank deeply, sickly sweet.

Clock over the sink: 4:30. Saturday afternoon. Nice going, Rockin' Joe.

"Hi," someone said brightly.

Joe spun around and saw this teenager seated at the raw kitchen table in front of the ornate cookstove.

"Ah, shit, scared me, boy!" He pulled his T-shirt down, snagged the kitchen towel hung sinkside. He covered himself, red and white checks, wished he hadn't cursed.

John Wayne voice: "There's a *real towel* in the bathroom there, pardner." The boy pointed, grinning. He was maybe fifteen, a small man, sitting stiffly upright, facing Joe squarely with his hands on the table on either side of a fat paperback book. His hair was short and dark, stiffly parted, damp with styling gel. His big dark eyes were steady and ironic, nose large, faintest ghost of a mustache, front teeth big and white in sidelong grin. He looked like his father. He looked like Tony, all right.

Joe sidled to the big bathroom, old tub in there, found a flowered beach towel and wrapped himself, long skirt. He stood tall to find some dignity, stepped back into the kitchen, said as conversationally as possible, "No water?"

"'No water?'" the boy growled, imitating him. "Nup! No water. There's something a little bit wrong with the *pump* again. Carl Andresen was supposed to come out yesterday to fix it, but the thing is, we forgot to pay him last time, so, well, the thing is, I don't think he's going to show up, do you?"

Long silence.

Joe said, "Got a piece of bread or something? That Kool-Aid . . ."

"Look in the breadbox. We got no Irish or Scottish, but we might have *English* muffins, but then, there's no gas, so you can't cook 'em."

"Where's the toaster?"

"Ha, ha, toaster! The toaster is toasted. And I don't feel like making a fire. You'll have to eat it, you know, kind of *raw*."

Joe found the English muffins in the genuinely gorgeous bread box as the kid piped on: "I made that box—well, not really—my father and me made that box, it's *rosewood*, that's why it's so *groovy*, like the neck of a really good guitar. You're a musician?"

"That's right."

"And you're hungover as *anything*?" He leaned forward, with a direct and eager gaze.

"That, I'm afraid, is right."

"And you snorfed a lot of strange powders last night?"

"No, kid, I did not."

"Oh, whoa! 'Kid.' *I'm* cool! Say no to *drugs*, kid." The boy broke into hilarious laughter, fully aware of his power to irritate. He turned his book, *Dune,* over and stared intently at Joe. "And you slept with Connie, right? 'Cuz I heard you."

Slowly: "Ah, hey, I'm sorry, man."

"You know how I knew you were a *musician*?"

Politely: "You want to chill out a little?"

The boy lowered his voice to an extravagant whisper. "'Cuz Connie only likes to boink musicians. Once a month. You're right on schedule. You're in the Rockin' Joe Heath band?"

Humbly: "I *am* Rockin' Joe Heath."

"Oh! Well! Aren't you *special*." Some tag line from a TV show. "*Bing*! She got the leader this time! How'd you like her?" The boy whooped loud as hell. "Is she pretty *sassy*?"

Joe remembered a quick scene from the night, something on the staircase, the inseams of Connie's blue jeans where they joined, her laughter. "Cut it out," he said. "I know she's your mom. You're Jesse, right? I used to play with your father back in the Blues Machine days. I knew you when you were a stinking peanut."

Mock fan, head bobbing in pretend sympathy, fingers under chin: "How come you're not famous anymore, Rockin'?"

Joe shrugged, opened the refrigerator again, looked in. Nothing to drink. He shut the door softly, turned to face the boy: "I'm sorry about your dad."

Comically solemn face: "Say-no-to-drugs."

Joe bit into the dusty English muffin, took a swig of the red bug juice. Four years since Anthony "Gui-tar" DeAngelis died. Connie said last night she still can't listen to a Neil Young record, since Neil Young was headliner on the tour, and nothing of Tony's and certainly none of the Blues Machine albums. Not even the radio, just in case. The thought of Paris makes her nervous, or furious, or ill.

Rockin' Joe coughed. His hangover made everything seem particular, segmented, unflowing. The kid's weird teasing and clowning brought nothing but sorrow, a flood from the past: lost auditoriums, band fights, airports, bus trips, lights in the face, and high as hell always. The kid continued to stare, making comical faces in imitation of Joe's chewing.

Just like Tony: always goofing.

Joe felt himself flush like he hadn't ever. He said, "Your mom and I have been friends a long, long time," and took another swig of the bug juice.

"She looks beautiful, huh? She's only thirty-four."

"Beautiful." Joe turned away.

The kid turned serious: "It's all right. She's my mom, but she's also like my best friend or my roommate or something." He flipped *Dune* over and pretended to read, then looked up. "Did you ever read this book? It's *awesome*. You ought to hang around today, stay for dinner and all. I mean, it's Saturday, right? And watch a movie on the VCR, we got plenty of movies, and the electricity is on for sure."

"I got to get back to New York."

"This *is* New York, you big nack-nack, the nice part of New York. And you don't have a car, anyway, I couldn't help but notice."

Rockin' Joe laughed. The boy was like a comedian, rapid delivery, raised eyebrows, drumming on the table to accent his punch lines: "We've got four hundred acres. Go get dressed and I'll take you for a walk, all right? But don't expect much. It's kind of a mess since summer. I mean, I've got to go to school, don't I? We sold all the cows, but there's still the llama you could see. And we got pumpkins! Don't worry. It's a weekend. Mom'll sleep till it's dark."

"Has she been all right? Where are the girls? I hear you've got sisters now."

"Who? Maggot and Hairball? Granma D's got 'em in Ithaca for the weekend, so Mom can have some fun." Bap de bap on the table. A mighty whoop. "Fun. That's you."

Joe turned and looked out the window over the sink. The glass was old, bubbled and ridged, and it made the long field of corn stubble out there stretch and jump as he rocked his head. Connie must rent the fields to farmers. At the end of the near pasture was a hedgerow of mature maples filled with dead branches, red at their tops, yellow halfway, deep green toward the ground, flamingly bright in clear sun. Joe waggled the single handle of the sink faucet. "No stinking water," he muttered. "No stinking shower."

"You'll stinking live. You're Stinkin' Joe Heath!"

There was something so comic about this kid, the way he flipped his hands around, the parody of Joe's hungover mug, that Joe laughed with him now, laughed harder and harder, deep snorts of laughter, the kid not exactly laughing along but imitating Joe's laughter: hiccups of laughter, bent-double laughter.

Suddenly Joe choked and gagged, burped, coughed. Mortifyingly, a little acid-pink Kool-Aid splashed on the floor. Joe froze, afraid of more. His towel dropped around his bare feet.

"Oh, man! You are *disgusting*," Jesse said. He flipped *Dune* back over and began to read.

Joe retrieved his towel only slowly, wiped his mouth with it, and dropped it over the small red puddle he had made. "It's that stinking bug juice."

Jesse did not look up. He said, "Yeah, right. Like you didn't drink four quarts of Jack Daniel's last night. I mean, how old are you, anyway?"

Joe turned to the sink, rattled the faucet handle with small violence. "No fucking water," he growled. The taste in his mouth—*hell*.

"You need a bath," Jesse said, so tenderly. Catching himself, he raised his eyebrows—Groucho Marx—did another drum roll on the table. "Why don't you go get your pants? I mean. I'll take you down to the pond. You could swim."

"Jesus, boy," Joe said, meaning, Let's not wake up your mom. If he saw Connie again, he might never leave.

Jesse said, "Okay. Just hang out. I'll get your pants for you." He sprang up and darted out of the room before Joe could protest, pounded up the stairs.

Three kids, farm and home. That would be the end of Rockin' Joe. Connie, Connie, Constance. He remembered her, suddenly, in the Blues Machine reunion crowd at The Rongo last night, big surprise that she would show up at all, diffident and streaky blonde at the side of the raging dance floor, big complicated eyes, her cheeks pink from uncharacteristic drinking. Okay, no surprise, though on the phone she'd said, "Forget it, Joe, forget it." Said she would not be in town. Said she had no taste for crowds. Said she had no wish for music, and not the Blues Machine, not that. Forget it, forget it, forget it. But there in the crowd she held this slight smile, and you would have thought nothing bad had ever happened to her, the peaceful way she bobbed her head, just the slightest nod, to the loud music. Rockin' Joe, he'd sung two ballads to her from the stage, not really kidding, then looked for her in the crush, first break. She was hanging out up by the bar with a couple of local bikers—serious guys— talking intently, her hand on a hairy forearm and cobra tattoo, listening intently, as well. She knew the tender side of everybody. Joe got the message, didn't approach. The little place was packed. Years since the Blues Machine had played together, more since they'd played someplace so small, more yet since they'd played here, those early days, Tony DeAngelis still in *college*. Next set, Joe sang every song to Connie, and then in the break they got to talk out on the fire escape over the creek where once they'd all done dope with Tony. You name it. You stinking name it. Talk: Connie was back teaching ceramics at TC3, that earnest little Tompkins County Community College. She still thought Joe should shave his beard, to show his chin again. She had new lines at her eyes that suddenly were the most beautiful thing about her. Joe was smitten all over, listening: her studio, in a storefront right on the main street of Trumansburg, was going strong, had become a hangout for what amounted to the arts scene and the women's movement in the little town. There was no profit in the place, but Connie would never give it up. She had her wheels in there, and her slab roller and two gas kilns. She'd bought an ornate little woodstove for the gallery she kept open in the front of the place, where her pals put their feet up like farmers (some of them *were* farmers) and drank coffee and talked whole days away, where nothing ever sold. Her kids were fine, she said. Joe asked for a kiss, actually asked for a kiss before he went back on, but she wouldn't quite let him, didn't quite not, either, gave him her cheek. All that was over, she said into his neck. Rockin' Joe called a lot of ballads in the last set, sang them for her alone, like no one else was in the room, no old fans, no young women, no couples dancing slow. He was as in love with Connie as ever. And despite the crowded room and the music all around him, Old Wally's sweet sax, Angel's deep bass, the Wonder Women singing backup, the Blues Machine was dead.

The boy pounded down the steps, spun into the kitchen, flung Joe's pants in his face. "She's out like a tree stump," he said. "You must have spronked her really, really well."

"I told you to chill on that stuff." Joe pulled his pants on and followed Jesse out the back door, shoeless. The sun was hot through the cool air, perfect September evening. Time for school to begin, new starts of all kinds. The sky was clear as the kind of drunken high in which Joe would stare at something hard and seem to see it through a perfect tunnel of understanding. Time to quit all that. He stood and breathed, felt better, looking around: leaves already falling, dervish whirls in gusty breezes, grass too high on what should have been a lawn. A sweeping spruce tree rose sixty feet, perfect cone in front of the house, swaying with those breezes, creaking with them by the gravel road. The melancholy perfection of the place overcame Joe: cry for Tony! Cry for Connie! Cry for maybe everyone on this sad planet, where people come and go and only live so long. Cry and then hit the road, Joe thought. Back to New York. He'd better get his ass down to the club, he best. The show was over, it was done.

"The pond's back here," Jesse called. "There's no llama, though. I was l-lying." He started off, but Joe stood transfixed by a hose coiled sloppily on the side of the two-kiln garage.

"I got to get some kind of a drink here." He put the nozzle to his lips, held the hose up high. A slight wash of warm, hose-flavored water fell into his mouth: not horrible. He swished and spat, held up another coil, another meager drink. Jesse helped him then, pulling the hose free and holding up coils. Not enough to wash up, but enough to get rid of the rotten taste of old Kool-Aid in his mouth.

"Let's *boogie*," Jesse said, savoring the prehistoric phrase, something his old man would have said. He led Joe over potsherds and broken firebricks and several bent Barbie dolls to an old cart path that ran between two stone walls and two noble and gnarled rows of old maples, path and walls and trees separating two good fields. Connie had propped fractured and underfired vases and pitchers against the tree trunks and along the tops of the rocks, colorful and meaningful in the lowering day. The cart path needed clearing; saplings had begun to choke it, threatened the older trees. Plenty work here.

"Now these are sugar maples," said Rockin' Joe Heath. "You can take the sap and make syrup and candy and stuff."

"My father used to say that, too, but he never did it."

"You boil it down, and boil it down."

Seriously: "How old are you?"

"I'm forty-three. How old are you?"

"Oh, fifteen, and that's the thing. I'm going to college before too long, you know? I'm going to want to get out of here." He looked at

Joe significantly, then marched ahead. He stopped. "You play guitar? Or what?" He was back into his comedy routine, wiggling his arms, dancing ahead in the leaves, making faces.

Joe laughed. "I'm a singer, and you stinking know it."

"I play guitar, but I like to write, too, and draw. And you stinking know it!"

"You ought to think about being a comedian or an actor or something."

"Well, I've certainly got the looks for it!" Jesse tweaked his own cheeks, then ran ahead, darted through an opening in the wall, and disappeared.

Joe shuffled behind him carefully, barefoot in the leaves, not quite warm enough, that hangover sweeping back in. The trees beside the cart path formed a tunnel that stretched straight ahead to a view of the sky over the top of a distant ridge. He remembered laughing in a car, in a back seat. Gator's car, it was, the new goddamn guitarist. Connie was funny. Right. Connie was really funny, made everyone laugh when she wanted to, laughing straight up the long hill to the house. This was supposed to have been just a ride home for her, but Wally and Gator had pushed Rockin' Joe out behind her in her driveway and peeled out, that old trick, like they were kids. And Joe thought he'd better thank the boys, except the one thing: now he was stuck.

He and Connie had laughed it up in the driveway, ending up kissing like old times sitting on the back stoop under starlight, half-frozen. And it wasn't like they had never made love before, or like they weren't in love still. She must have been just as drunk as he was. In the house he'd played the piano and sung with her, and they had kissed on the bench and had a regular riot, and the bench fell over and they lay on the floor—right—no wonder the kid woke up. Joe felt rotten thinking of Jesse having to hear them. He remembered the pink dawn that was in all the windows when he and Connie finally got off the staircase and into her room. They never even took their shirts off. Right. She didn't want her shirt off. Joe shuffled down the cart path in the leaves, the night coming clear in his mind, and older times, too, the gigs at the Jersey Shore, Connie's new baby and her obsessive concern about appearing in her bikini—stretch marks—that would be fifteen years past. He remembered her before Jesse, too, and before Tony, remembered her at that first blues festival in Vermont. Then, unbidden thought, he remembered what the older musicians seemed like back then, bald guys trying to act like kids, trying to impress the kids, and only the other old bald guys liked them, and some of the girls of course. The best of the girls, come to think of it. Joe shook his head and shuffled in the leaves. Christ if he hadn't just last week colored his graying hair with black, black rinse.

At the break in the wall a lesser trail led downhill through long grass and brambles a couple hundred yards to the rippling pond, Jesse's path through the fallen leaves plain enough. And there Jesse was, still goofily running, flailing his arms like a much younger kid, windmilling his arms and whooping his way to a wooden dock that had long since rotted and fallen into the water. A skin of bubbling, vile algae on the pond's surface stretched out from the little beach that someone had made by clearing reeds and spreading sand. The only clear water was on the other side, no way to get to it through the reedy swamp that formed most of the pond's shore. "Looks like I'm not going to get to swim," Joe said.

"I'll give you twenty bucks if you go in."

"Keep it. We didn't even bring a towel."

"All right, then. I'll give you twenty bucks if you fix the pump." Jesse pointed to a tall doghouse of a building. "Unless it just needs to be primed. That's what Carl always does. Then I'll only give you a quarter. Oh. And we lost the key."

"Well, I can prime a pump all right."

After a long and silent gaze at the pond and at the trees and the hills and the streaky sky, Jesse watching him, Joe pushed his way through brambles to study the sturdy little pump house, built over what looked to be a hand-dug artesian well. The door was absurdly padlocked. Jesse ran up beside him, stood too close, a comic examination of the lock.

Joe said, "We can just clobber it till it pops, easy enough. Could you maybe run and go get a couple of tools? Crescent wrench and a hammer? And some kind of bucket ? And a screwdriver. And maybe pliers?"

Jesse made a loopy face of pretend concentration, rushed suddenly backwards through the brambles, then backwards up the path, looking intently at Joe, full-speed amazing backwards. Joe smiled, gave Jesse his laughter, pointed at him and laughed hard for him, laughed till the boy twirled twice at the stone wall and sprinted toward the house.

Beautiful, beautiful land here. Joe held the padlock bright and cold in his hand, studied it for several long minutes, whiskey-induced particularity of vision, grew dizzy. Dizzy, dizzy, too much fun. He dropped the lock and stretched his arms to hold the little pump house, lay his bearded cheek on the rough warm shingles of its roof. His head swam. He was a fool, a waste, a has-been, a nothing, a drunk, a clown: Grecian Formula, fuck. He hadn't been this sick from drinking for years. What was he thinking? What could he ever do for Connie? Up all night, the two of them, like twenty-five. Tequila *after* whiskey. And where did that big bag of oranges come from? He was someone Connie loved. She said so, at least that. He saw her over him, still wearing her black Harley Davidson T-shirt, her hair falling blonde into his face, leaving a tunnel in the dawn to her dark eyes. It was those dark eyes with the blonde hair that made her so lovely to him, he thought. It was those dark eyes with the blonde hair and the subtle laugh and the careful analytic conversation and her ability to feel and offer joy, and that undertow of honest sorrow. And for that many hours he'd felt something different from this darkness he walked around with, not even knowing he walked with it till now. Connie had done that for him in the past, too. But this kid Jesse. And Maggie and Harriet, little girls he had never met. Quite a package, Tony's legacy. Joe held the pump house tighter to prop himself, twitched a couple of times and fell asleep.

He woke when his grip loosened and his face slid down the little roof, the shingle stones pulling at his beard, woke with a violent start, released his hug on the house.

Jesse handed him tools. "Here's the hammer. Didn't want to wake you. Mom's still in z-land, too; you set the record, Rockin' Joe Heath!" He dropped the other tools, beat his thin chest, yodeled like Tarzan.

Annoyed: "Chill, man." Joe wasted no time, swung the hammer, tapped the padlock precisely. It sprang open. Jesse clapped his hands and hissed breathily to imitate big-auditorium applause, very convincing. Joe grinned despite himself at this teasing, at first hiding it, but then he looked up to give the grin to Jesse. He felt gauzy but remarkably better after his tiny upright nap.

The pump house door fell open. Joe reached inside past spider webs to snap the perfectly modern breaker bar in there and cut the electricity to the ungodly ancient motor. He stared at the piping, at the electric heater, at the old iron wheel and belt of the pump. "This is an incredibly stupid setup," he said.

"That's what Carl says."

"I mean, check it out. Why not sink a pump in the goddamn well? And they got to have a heater in here, for Christ's sake. What happens to this thing in the winter? Hand me a wrench."

Jesse patted Joe's palm with the big old adjustable wrench twice, took it back twice, ha ha. He said, "My father built this whole thing. And he dug the well his self, too, the whole thing. And restored the pond, which was just a mudhole then."

"It's not so bad." Joe poked around the base of the pump in the dark, unscrewed a bolt, retightened it, tried another. There was no room to reach in, really, and the door ledge pressed on his chest painfully. He said, "Oh, it's not so bad at all," knocking his knuckles against the greasy metal of the pump motor. "And the stone work down below here looks awfully nice. Must have been quite a project. Your old dad was more a mason than a plumber, maybe."

"I helped him, at least a little. I was four?"

"Four," Joe said. "We're messing with first memories here!"

Long silence, Joe feeling his way along the base of the pump.

In some kind of robot voice Jesse said, "My first memory, if you want to know, is actually the *band*, Joe, you guys really, really loud on a stage outside somewhere with Hell's Angels and a big giant crowd dancing and me on Mommy's shoulders and *I didn't like it*."

That last delivered like another punch line, but not at all funny, not one bit. Joe kept probing, and at last, in the most inaccessible spot possible, back edge of the old pump body, his fingers found the priming port. Fighting the wrench in there, slipping off the nut repeatedly, grunting, stretching his arms, pulling then pushing that wrench in no room at all, he finally managed to loosen the threaded plug, back it out, and not drop it or the wrench He stuck his pinky in the port to be sure he had it right.

"Now we need some water," he said, extricating himself.

Jesse had brought the Kool-Aid pitcher and not a bucket—good enough—raced to the pond to fill it. Joe poured that water into the little threaded opening, slowly, six pitchers full, Jesse a whirlwind getting more. Finally, the port gurgled and overflowed. Joe screwed the threaded plug back in (not too tight—someone would be doing this again soon), pulled his beard, twice, hoping he'd done the priming right, then hit the breaker. The old pump jumped to life. The trickle pipe that fed the pond began to drip, then to flow, lightly.

"Showers!" said Joe, exultant. His feet were freezing.

"Cold showers," Jesse told him seriously. "No gas. Mom did a firing Wednesday and used up the tank. End of savings! Doom and destruction!"

Walking back to the house in the shuffling leaves, Jesse kept pace with Joe, no clowning. The sun wasn't far from setting, long shadows, wind now, and cold.

Jesse said it again: "How come you're not famous anymore?"

Joe pushed his collar up. He said, "I do all right."

Jesse pushed on: "But I never hear of you at all anymore. I mean, you're still on the road. You're still playing at little bars. I thought you old guys kicked back and wrote songs or something."

"I thought so, too, chief."

Silence.

"And wait a minute—I do write songs. Lots and lots of songs. They're on the stinking radio."

"Mom always says how he shouldn't have fired you. She told Carter and Betty the other night all about it, 'cuz they said you were coming back for the reunion."

"Your mom likes me, Jess." Laughing in the window seat, her room, some kind of extended trouble with buttons, serious dark eyes suddenly—kissing again.

"She thinks you're *so* handsome," the boy said, imitating her inflections perfectly. He tried to keep clowning, but this was serious: "I was just kidding about the musician every month, Rockin' Joe. And I knew you were you. Also, she's thirty-eight."

"I know how old she is."

"Were you ever married or anything?"

Joe laughed. "Who would marry me?" He looked at Jesse, saw how the boy's jaw rose strongly back to his ear like Connie's.

"Are you the one she used to visit in New York?"

Joe shrugged, embarrassed: "Maybe so."

"Just maybe every weekend for a year."

"Your dad was gone, Jess."

They stopped walking. There was the house, right there, that big old spruce tree. A new shot of wind came, hard chill, bearing leaves from the maples, flapping Jesse's big shirtsleeves. Joe's bare feet all of a sudden were bricks of ice, prickly, fucked.

Jesse said, "There's never time to get things done around here. I mean I'm in school, and I'm a teenager, I'm not going to do much, am I? What's more useless than a teenager? There's a ton of insurance money someplace, if you think that's the problem. It's *invested*. And you know what? My dad grew thirty thousand dollars worth of pot here one year."

Joe raised a doubtful eyebrow, fought the old bad feeling. He knew the band bus had left with the equipment, knew no one had thought or cared to come get him. His fading Jaguar was on the street in Trumansburg, safe enough. "I got to get out of here," he said. "I really do."

"Well, you're going to have to walk. Granma D's got the car."

"With the little girls."

Teen irony, full force: "That's right, Rockin'!"

"So what's on the VCR tonight?" Joe said, picking up the joke. He could walk to Hall's Corners, hitch from there.

Jesse, suddenly sincere: "Actually, I lied. We don't have a VCR. We don't even have a TV. Sorry. But we got stuff to make *lasagna*, we really do, and Mom's got a jug of wine, okay? I'll read to you from *Dune* or something. And make a huge fire."

Joe got a picture of Connie much younger, not so different from now, Connie nineteen at her wheel throwing these perfect pots, one after the next, turning them, shaping them while he watched, amazed. Just that, a picture from the past.

"I got to get back to New York," Joe said finally. "Thanks, though." He could still split before Connie woke—poor Connie, never a great partyer, way out of practice—and that would be that, the perfect goodbye.

Joe patted Jesse's shoulder a couple of times, then back to the house in a hurry, frozen feet.

Jesse raced to gather a huge pile of sticks from the lawn, brought them in by the stove, rushed out to load himself with logs from the tumbled woodpile. Joe held the screen door for him, didn't let it slam, danced a little on the cold tile floor as he entered the kitchen. He wanted his socks and shoes—time to hike on out of here—but he didn't want to wake Connie, and the shoes were in her room. He made a few false starts toward the stairs. Forget it.

Abruptly, he remembered his pump project, went to the sink. The faucet sputtered and coughed and bubbled, spat some rusty sludge, ran rusty two minutes, muddy two more, then clear, good, cold water, flowing well, time a-wasting. And once again Joe grinned despite himself, pleased as hell with his success, watched the water, put his hands in it, drank, washed his face, dunked, lifted his dripping head, saw out the window when he opened his eyes that the dusk had begun to descend, pink as the dawn.

Jesse banged around at the old woodstove, building his fire as noisily as possible. Joe thought how you might just sit down there at the table, put your feet up close to the stove. Jesse's flames leapt up out of the cook rings. The boy knew what he was doing. Joe's feet—two stinking ice bricks. To walk would warm them. Hustle down the hill to Hall's Corners, put out his thumb. He leaned back on the sink as if relaxed, said, "Hey, maybe you could get my shoes and socks for me upstairs there, Jess, what d'ya think?"

"Okay. But maybe you want to take a bath before you go."

"Can't."

Jesse, entreating: "Take a bath before you go." No kidding around, now. "I'll heat some water here. You can take a nice hot bath. You're shivering anyway." He looked to the ceiling, looked to Joe, began again to clown, noisily as hell searched the cabinets to find his mom's gargantuan canning kettle, then two large buckets and two smaller pots, bumping them into everything, clang and bang to fill them at the sink then splash to the stove, pushing Joe out of the way, one vessel at a time, big groan heaving each to its circle of fire in the blackened cooktop. The ritual did not seem new to Jesse. He put more wood in the fire, which was already raging.

Rockin' Joe Heath stepped through Jesse's puddles to the table and sat, put his feet up on a chair, let them burn in the heat. He picked up *Dune* and read from Jesse's place in it, waiting. Giant worms, strange planet. Another hour wouldn't matter. And Jesse wasn't going for any shoes. The stove was hot, the boy quiet.

Quickly, the water in the smaller pots began to steam, then to bubble and boil. Soon after that—big fire—the buckets, too. The water in the big canning kettle took longer, never quite boiled, but rolled a little, and steamed. Joe pretended to read, even turned pages, saw himself starting the Jag in T-burg, New York City a long drive, five hours.

Jesse made four fast trips across the nicely overheated kitchen, splashing into the bathroom to fill the claw-foot tub, avoiding the hot spills. Joe heard him adding cold water from the tap. "Your bath," Jesse announced. He had folded a towel over his arm and bowed like a small, worried butler.

Joe stood and undressed where he was, old hippie, leaving his clothes in a simple pile on the kitchen floor. He walked naked past

Jesse into the big bathroom—lots of hand-done tile work—slipped into the tub, sighed, lay back. The boy had surely got the temperature right. Jesse smiled happily, watching Joe, clanged the canner and the buckets and pots back for more water, more fire. Joe heard the clank of the firebox door: get that thing roaring. And about when the bath was going chilly, Jesse reappeared, bearing buckets. Joe closed his eyes and let the boy pour the water over him. Jess went back for the smaller pots, poured those.

"Save that big one for yourself," Joe said.

Jess banged off with the buckets and pots, filled them at the sink, put them on the stove, panting with the effort of carrying so much water, no clowning.

Joe stood when the water went cold again, stood wrinkled and wasted, took himself a quick cold shower, drained the tub, rinsed it for the boy.

He called, "Get ready, Jess," wrapped himself in a worn Barbie beach towel. Jesse undressed quickly, demure, as Joe stepped dripping into the hot kitchen to fetch the boiling new batches of water one vessel at a time. And Joe filled the tub, adjusted the temperature with the very cold water from the well Jesse's dad had dug. Jesse, child again, poured Mr. Bubble and climbed into the tub in his underpants. He splashed and goofed while Joe in his swinging towel filled pots, brought them to the stove.

And Rockin' Joe stoked the fire, turned the pots, breathed in steam, stood in warm puddles tending his chore, the kitchen a sauna. When the smallest pots were hot enough—not long—he carried them to the bath, poured the water over Jesse, two buckets next, huge kettle last, a very long bath. Jesse splashed and sang and dunked himself, blew bubbles, splashed and sang.

Joe kept moving, clang and bong of the pots, put more water on—let the kid soak all night!—stoked the fire even more, sat down in the great heat at the table and opened *Dune*, read a little, thinking lasagna didn't sound half bad, thinking how in one of these pots here he'd boil the noodles shortly, layer 'em up in cheese and sauce, let the fire burn down for baking, glass of wine. He stood twice to check the water. The third time he rose he heard Connie coming down the stairs. Joe bumped in a rush past the table, losing his towel. He lunged for his pants and shirt, picked them up fast, but they were soaked. That left him pretty well naked and barefoot in a puddle, keeping back big laughter, holding his bundle of dripping clothes. And right away Connie was there in the doorway, surprised, her hair awry, her bathrobe open over the Harley T-shirt, her cheeks rising into her dark eyes as she grinned at the mess.

She said, "Joe?"

A Job at Little Henry's

Richard Milk thought about the stolen money all weekend, planned different speeches, different ways of dealing with Dewey Burke on Tuesday when Dewey was due to show up. Richard wanted to explode in Dewey's pocked face, but yelling wasn't going to work. Better to quietly ask that jailbird to admit the theft, then offer to let him work it off, solemnly hear his promises, and maybe no longer allow him in the house.

Such were Richard's thoughts all weekend—a long weekend, as it happened, Richard following Gail to no fewer than six Memorial Day picnics and dinners and dances—the problem of Dewey Burke crowding into every crevice left by more immediate concerns. And, in truth, Richard found these thoughts of Dewey something of a relief, this new trouble much easier to think about than Lester Molina or the rocky going of late with Gail.

Late Monday night, Richard moved the money jar out of the kitchen, put it in Gail's desk, put a few bucks in it to get it started again. That ridiculous money jar—the habit of a twenty-two-year marriage. Right now, they were trying to put together enough spare dimes and quarters and dollar bills and occasional fives to buy a good chunk of next year's spring trip to Florida.

On Tuesday, Memorial Day weekend was over and Gail went to work. She was the area coordinator in School Administrative District 98, LaDoux County, Maine, which meant that she and Richard were comfortable enough, despite his recent troubles: Richard was out of work. Up until six weeks ago he'd been chief designer at Molina Log Homes, an enormous prefabricating operation that Molina had started in his back-to-the-land days. Now it was a small empire, stretching across the top of America clear to Montana. Richard had designed every home they marketed, designed them for beauty, designed them for comfort, designed them for the earth-friendly aspects Molina Log Homes advertised, designed them for profit, too, and so that logs could be shipped pre-cut aboard ever smaller trucks. Lester had talked lugubriously for an hour about housing starts and the shaky economy, but his theatrically sad eyes couldn't hide what had really happened: Richard Milk had drawn all the designs Lester Molina needed to do his huge business forever, and so Lester had let him go.

Oh, yes, on Tuesday the long weekend was over. Richard stood in the yard an hour after breakfast (Gail long gone in her safe red Saab), just stood and looked at the hills across the way. The thief Dewey turned up exactly on time. Richard saw him coming up the road, slouching up the road with his bouncing reform-school swagger. Richard felt calm, told himself a few encouraging words, tried a sentence out: *I'll understand if you don't want to admit it right away, but . . .*

Then the bum was at the door, saying it was a decent day—in fact, saying just those words, with no inflection at all, no way to sense the man: "Decent day."

"Nice 'un," Richard said. "Yup." He found himself talking the way Dewey did, just as he'd found himself talking like the Koreans he'd met in the city, just as he'd found himself talking like Texans when he and Gail lived down there. Gail saw this cultural echolalia (that was the phrase she used, sometimes gently, usually not) as a lack of boundaries, as the symptom of a man with no self. Richard saw it as his quite firm self's private brand of mockery, something he did unconsciously to nearly everyone, especially people he regarded as less sophisticated. In any case, it was something he meant to cut out.

Dewey had no more conversation in him, turned and walked back around the house to the shed, pulled out a shovel and rake, and headed over to the corner of the woodlot to continue exactly where he'd left off the Thursday before, digging out the old compost, putting it cartload by cartload on the garden. Richard followed him more slowly, choosing words: *But don't worry, we understand, we know a call for help when we hear it. You've worked for us faithfully for over a year. You won't be fired. We only want . . .* what? What did they want? Gail hadn't seemed the least bit concerned. "We'll have to get rid of him," was all she said, meaning that Richard had to get rid of him, of course.

"Dewey?"

"Mister?"

"Dewey, there's something I want to talk to you about."

"Right."

"Dewey, we're concerned. You've offended our trust. Let me put it bluntly: Gail and I know you stole our money." That didn't sound right—too confrontational. "Dewey, this really . . . pisses me off. You stole from us."

"Didn't either."

"Dewey, you stole forty-five dollars on Tuesday and fourteen on Thursday."

"The fuck I did." Dewey stabbed the shovel into the compost and straightened, looked square at Richard. His eyes were as cold and deep and dark as the quarry ponds in Avon to which Richard and Gail had made the strenuous hike last summer with the intention of swimming. They had not swum. The place was beautiful and what one once thought of as secluded, the water green and clear and very deep, but there were too many beer cans and lots of trash and diapers and those grotesque, mud-splattered off-road trucks parked halfway up the sides of boulders for show and too many people who looked like Dewey Burke, people like Dewey everywhere, a circus of tattoos and hidden weaponry.

Something firmer: "Dewey, listen, you're caught. Now if you'd just take a minute to think about it . . . I mean, you're caught. We caught you. You stole our money. Dewey, listen to me. You stole from us."

The look on Dewey's face went cloudy, then black. He stepped toward Richard and swung his arm—that's what Richard saw, the arm. The tattooed fist seemed to arrive separately, and too early, arrived right at Richard's nose and sent him into a vague and fuzzy time warp in which everything Dewey did seemed extremely slow and purposeful, almost inevitable, certainly unstoppable. Richard didn't fall, didn't take a fighter's stance, just put a hand to his face in amazement. "Jesus, Dewey." And that fist came back, hitting Richard's hand, knocking his own soft palm into his own hard cheekbone. "That's enough."

"Don't tell *me*," Dewey spouted, and he swung again, this time hitting Richard's eye so precisely that the fist (tattooed B-A-D-D across the knuckles) blocked the light for a moment. A strong punch to his stomach (L-U-C-K) finally knocked Richard down.

Dewey stopped. "You say sorry," he said. "Say it." He loomed over Richard, threatening with his marked fists as Richard sat up.

"Jesus, Dewey."

Dewey whirled—some kind of homespun martial-arts move—whirled and kicked Richard in the side. Richard's ribs made a deep internal crunch, and hurt sharply, so he lay down. Dewey kicked him again, this time on the butt, then once more, sharply on the thigh. "Sacka shit," Dewey said. He stood over Richard a moment, waiting for the slightest twitch, a single word, the tiniest reason to resume the beating, then seemed to decide that Richard was through and walked off with the same slow swaggering slouch as always.

〉 〉 〉

The sheriff's deputy who turned up late in the afternoon sat in his car for five minutes talking on the radio, only opened his door when Richard came out of the house. By now both of Richard's eyes were black, and of course his nose hurt. He didn't think his ribs were broken, but he'd begun to consider a call to Dr. LeMonteau (pronounced locally as Lemon Toe) to ask about his leg, which ached deeply, ached to the bone. Gail wasn't going to believe this.

"Looking good," the deputy said, swinging his legs out of the car but remaining seated. He pulled a thick notepad from his shirt pocket, produced a pen.

"Thank you," Richard said.

"Dewey Burke's one tough rabbit, sir. I'd think twice about fighting him again."

"I wasn't *fighting* him. He attacked me. Right back there. Punched me over and over, kicked me in the leg, knocked me down, all because I confronted him about some money he'd stolen." Into Richard's voice crept the clipped quality of the deputy's. He tried to cut it out: "He stole money from us in two days of work: forty-five dollars the first time—we hoped maybe it had just been misplaced— fourteen the second time, which is when I decided to talk to him about it."

The deputy put on a practiced skeptical frown. He hadn't written a word on his pad. "You have proof he stole it?"

"Well, of course. He was the only one here. Both Tuesday and Thursday."

"Your kids didn't take it?"

"The kids are in college, sir, both of them."

"You keep your doors locked?" The deputy had a cast to his eye, seemed to be looking over Richard's shoulder.

"Well, not generally, not when we're around, of course. Probably seldom. Mostly just when we're away."

"So anyone could have come right in and took the money, correct?"

"But who on earth would do that?"

"Drug addicts."

Richard wearily smiled, gave a good-natured shake of his head: "You're getting a little outlandish, sir."

"Friends of your kids, maybe."

Richard struggled to stay calm. Here in rural Maine his children had found themselves viewed negatively as artsy types, and the deputy would certainly know that fact, know exactly how long Ricky's hair was, and see in his mind the many colors of Cindy's tie-dyed shirts, see the kids' sweet bunch of friends gathered playing Frisbee in the little park near the County Court Building. "My children's friends are among the most honest in town, Mr. Springer."

"Just borrowing a few bucks, maybe. Don't get weepy—I'm just looking for the facts here, and the facts is you don't have any evidence that Dewey Burke stole anything whatsoever at all."

Richard had learned to stay quiet a minute when insulted or angry, and so he did, stood quietly, looking away from the deputy, who looked away from him, still holding his unpoised pen and his empty pad, still making no sign that he'd get out of the car to investigate.

Finally Richard said, "Let's get to the point. I was attacked. A dangerous felon is loose."

"Would you like to press charges?"

"Do I need to press charges?"

"Well, in the case of fights, generally, we won't make an arrest unless there's been property damage."

"This wasn't a fight, Mr. Springer, as I've repeatedly told you."

"You mean you didn't get a single punch in?"

"I told you, sir, it was not a fight."

"Well. If you want to make a federal case out of it . . ." The deputy swung his legs back into the car, shut his door, sat staring out the windshield, seeming to try to decide whether to say what he was about to say. Then quietly, confidentially: "You'll want to know that if old Dew gets arrested for anything, anything at all, he's going back to jail for a wicked long time."

❭ ❭ ❭

Gail Milk got home late because of the monthly school board meeting, home to a darkened house. She found Richard on the kitchen floor holding his leg. Soon, in the emergency room at LaDoux County Hospital, they learned that he had suffered a hematoma, an intermuscular blood clot, which, as the doctor said, could certainly be painful, but which wasn't particularly dangerous, unless the clot were to loosen and travel through the chambers of Richard's heart and to his brain, where it would certainly kill him. Dr. LeMonteau said this was unlikely. Richard had two cracked ribs as well, not much to do for that, just rest and heal.

❭ ❭ ❭

Thursday morning, about the time Dewey would normally have appeared, a youngish woman came instead. Her hair looked partly washed. She appeared weary but intelligent, too, very bright in the eyes, something Richard was ashamed not to expect from inside a mobile home surrounded by old snow machines and car parts and doghouses. He tried hard not to notice her breasts, which were large and upstanding under her T-shirt, her nipples walleyed under the worn cloth. Her legs and hips were as unnaturally narrow as an undernourished child's. Dewey's girlfriend. Holding a rhubarb pie.

Richard accepted the pie as solemnly as it was offered, stood in the doorway holding it, facing the unpretty woman.

She spoke earnestly: "Mr. Milk, Dew says sorry for fucking you up. He's really sorry. But he just didn't steal from you and that's what got him off. He just didn't steal nothing. Never has. That's not his thing. And he's been in trouble plenty so when he's finally straightened out it just flipped him out. Know what I mean? God, you look awful."

"It's not so bad."

"So can he come back to work?"

⟩ ⟩ ⟩

Tuesday Dewey was back. He went immediately to the compost pile and resumed what he'd been doing a week past when Richard had confronted him: shoveling humus into the Milks' red yard cart. Richard watched from the kitchen window, remembering the woman and feeling himself to be a soft touch, sentimental even: he wanted to help Dewey, this thug in the garden. What was that all about? The man worked no faster or slower than he had before. He never looked up at the house, just shoveled the compost, wheeled the cart to the garden, spread the rich new earth. By midmorning he was done, had turned to the roto-tilling.

Normally, Dewey stopped for lunch—came up to the house, politely washed up at the kitchen sink, took the sandwich Richard offered, and ate it alone outside. Today he skipped lunch altogether.

He got the lawn mower out and paced the big lawn with it, stopping frequently to empty the bag of clippings into a new pile in the compost bin.

Richard tried to get to his studying. He meant to pass the architecture boards this fall. He'd failed twice out of grad school, then got the job with Molina and quit trying. The studying would comprise a full-time occupation till October. Richard sat at his drawing board and opened two books. He stared at the wall, stared at the pages of the books, put his face in his hands, pushed back in his chair, thought of inviting Dewey in for lunch, a little of what Gail liked to call *rapprochement*. He had to get a look at Dewey—make sure Dewey seemed all right. The man mowed the lawn in record time, stood sweating by the tool shed, making a cigarette with shreds of tobacco from his tattered pouch. Six dollars an hour wasn't much for all Dewey did. No wonder the poor guy was so full of fury.

Gail thought Richard was a fool, had said so during a heated exchange in the breakfast nook, "A fool and more of a masochist than I thought!"—but Richard wasn't going to back down this time. He felt something growing in him, felt he'd risen past revenge, transcended fear, had turned his other cheek, had experienced true compassion for the first time in all his days, something that arose in some way having to do with being fired, for sure, but something to do with Dewey's fists as well, something to do with the sharp points of Dewey's shoes.

"You are a dolt," Gail had said in anger (later she would apologize, with kisses). "A *dunderhead*. And you are deluding yourself. Get your architect's license—please!—pass that loser's exam, and then *get a job*, and you won't need to pay people to punish you for your *failures*!"

"You and your cheap psychology," Richard had replied. "Who's punishing whom around here?" But he would forgive Gail, too. He was capable of that.

❭ ❭ ❭

Alone at home on Saturday (Gail at a high-school track meet—her endless cheery obligations, the children far away at their respective wild college towns), Richard puttered a while, feeling cheerful, nearly healed. He whistled and felt positively euphoric, his turn at compassion having knocked depression from his shoulder.

He studied distractedly, drew buildings in the allotted ninety minutes while his oven timer ticked, drew based on what he knew the Regents of the Architecture Board would want to see. Richard worked despite himself till lunch, then stood in the yard looking at all Dewey had done. And suddenly, he had to see the man, take compassion past forgiveness to the next step: friendship. Richard felt the warm light of understanding surround him—he was not above Dewey; they had only had different luck in life. At length, he collected Dewey's lank girlfriend's untouched pie from the refrigerator, slid it from its pan (just a foil thing, not even the right size for a pie— probably saved from some frozen meal, Richard thought, then scolded himself), slid it into the compost bucket. He washed the tin: one needed an excuse for visiting along the Avon Road.

Pie tin in hand, Richard walked quickly down the road, suddenly aware of his new boating shoes, his bright socks, his purple shorts. Soon he was back in his house, searching his closet for clothes to wear to Dewey's. And in a black T-shirt from his son's drawer, blue jeans, workboots (both jeans and boots mortifyingly unscathed by work) Richard knocked on Dewey's trailer door. The knock was superfluous: four dark dogs straining at their chains bellowed Richard's presence, all bright teeth and rage.

Dewey had friends over. One of them, a large fellow in a clean shirt, came and blocked the door. "Yeah?" he said.

"I'm a neighbor," Richard said. "Just out walking around, thought I'd stop by, bring back this pie tin."

The man in the door looked him over.

Richard said, "Dewey here?"

"Dewey ain't."

The dogs barked hoarsely now, strangling themselves on their chained collars. Something was going on in the small living room behind the big fellow.

Dewey came up silently behind Richard, having somehow sneaked out of the trailer and come around the back side, startled him with a rough tap on the shoulder. Richard spun.

Dewey looked disgusted, said, "Oh, it's you."

"Yup. Me."

"You all better?"

"I'm okay, I guess." He gave a smile in anticipation of an apology, but an apology didn't come, and the men simply stood, a dooryard tableau, still as stumps. "I brought back your pie plate."

"Go in. Jim, s'okay."

The big man—Jim—stepped back. At the kitchen table a younger fellow hulked, staring. He had something hidden in his lap. Seeing Richard, seeing Dewey behind him, the kid breathed, relaxed, put two stout handguns on the table. Jim gave a flat laugh: huh huh huh. Richard noticed that the place was very clean, very tidy (cheaply furnished, to be sure), decent, nice.

"Have a sit," Dewey said.

Richard wanted to say no thanks, wanted to run out the door, but didn't want to appear to be shaken by the presence of the firearms, which were, after all, perfectly legal, so far as he knew. He said, "Going hunting?" This lame gambit turned out to be a hilarious joke, the laughter from Dewey and his pals long and hard and followed by a kind of formally granted but clearly temporary acceptance.

Dewey broke out a six-pack of Piels beer, and soon Richard was drinking his second can. By noon he was sharing yarns about college drinking exploits (these didn't seem as funny or racy as they did in other company), listening to yarns in turn. All three men were on parole, if you could believe what they said (Richard didn't, not really), and all three for violent crimes just short of murder. But they were funny, Richard thought, good at stories. How bad could they actually be? They were men operating without the benefit of education, without breaks, without hope. Barely aware how drunk he was becoming, Richard saw himself saving them. Compassion! They had a certain nobility, he began to think; they were almost saints.

Even drunk he could hear what Gail would say about that idea: These men are dangerous. Gail had always been blind that way, always blind, a snob. Richard rose, holding his beer can foaming in front of him. "I lost my job," he announced, a kind of toast.

Dewey nodded in real fellow feeling, sympathy Richard hadn't gotten yet from anyone.

So Richard went on, told the whole story: Molina's perfidy! The heartless phone call! The lousy severance package! The kids' college bills!

When Richard was done, the boys were with him 100 percent, pounded his back in sympathy, riffed a long time hilariously on the theme of destroying Lester Molina, rocked the table with their laughter, pictures of Molina filling the air of the trailer kitchen: Molina with his head in a toilet, his balls in a vise, his house on fire, his car in a pond.

At one o'clock the woman who'd delivered the pie came out of the back room carrying a little boy, four or maybe five or even six years old, too old, in any case, to need to be carried. But she never put him down. Impassive, she made plain whitebread sandwiches and held her boy and exerted a huge presence in the room in silence. The men only drank their beer while she worked, the conversation embarrassed to a halt in front of her.

So Richard said, "What's the boy's name?" He had drunk four beers.

No reply.

Richard tried again: "The kid, what's his name?"

"That's Don't He," big Jim said.

"What?"

"That's Don't He."

"Dewey and Don't He," the young man with the guns said, and he and Jim laughed.

"Don't he look like Dewey?" Jim said.

"Do he or don't he?" the young man—Baker—said.

Dewey said, "Leem alone," but his voice was mild; this wordplay was some kind of old joke.

"Don't He," Jim said one more time.

The woman put the sandwiches on the table. The child stayed in the crook of her arm. His mother didn't glower exactly, but the look on her face was no longer impassive. Something murderous was alive in her. She said, "He's Jeremy Charles, like his grandfather."

Richard said, "Hi, Jeremy," and the kid buried his face in his mother's neck.

She went back into the bedroom, closed the door.

The men ate. When his sandwich was gone, Richard began to think of graceful exit lines. Jim got up and went outside. Richard heard him piss, heard him open the door of his truck, cheered with the others when he saw the bottle of Old Granddad, though it didn't actually make him glad.

Later, Richard would puke on the side of the Avon Road, then again at the end of his driveway holding his sore ribs, then twice in his bathtub, where Gail would find him; but for now the afternoon stretched ahead, and the stories were good, and he enjoyed the company of what through his newfound compassion he'd revisualized suddenly as good men—rough men, surely, maybe not the smartest guys on the face of the earth, but men he chastised himself for misjudging.

❯ ❯ ❯

Dewey stopped coming to work. And because Dewey had no phone, it seemed to Richard after a couple of weeks that another visit to the trailer down the road was in order. He needed Dewey's help around the yard, he told himself. And he told Gail the same, when she said they were better off rid of Dewey forever: "You'd think he was your only friend," she said. "You'd think you didn't notice that he stole from us and beat your face and then made you sick with alcohol when you tried to reach out to him."

"Well, with your schedule I do need the company."

Gail sighed at this pale jest, this introduction of an old issue between them.

"Kidding," Richard said. "I'm only kidding. But really. I'm just going over to see if he wants work. I'll just go see him, that's all. I think the guy needs help. I think the guy *needs* me."

Gail hugged Richard with big teacherly warmth, said, "Well, fine. Go get Dewey. But don't come home barfing your guts out!" This last was the kind of joke she made to announce the end of an argument.

Richard laughed, remembering that day. Somehow the puking had given him a feeling of youth, had brought him back to a time when what was sensible didn't usually turn out to be what was right or needed.

So on a Saturday in July he dressed as a biker, left Gail to her preparations for that afternoon's 4-H luncheon, and headed on foot down

the Avon Road. He hoped Dewey would be home. He hoped big Jim
and Baker would be there. He hoped Jeremy Charles—Don't He—
would be there with his protective mom. And maybe today he'd have
a beer. Maybe today he'd have a beer and then another, and then as
much whiskey as Dewey. Who was to say he shouldn't? And maybe
today he'd make more of the jokes he'd made, and the guys would
laugh as they had before, and maybe tomorrow he'd be sick. Maybe
he would and what was wrong with that?

No one answered his knock at the trailer door. He waited,
knocked, and waited some more, then gave up. As he walked away,
Dewey tapped him on the shoulder, having appeared from nowhere
and silently behind him. When Richard turned, Dewey pretended
to hit him with a left, L-U-C-K, then stabbed him with a pretend
knife in a tightly squeezed right. Dewey didn't smile. A normal person would smile after a joke like that, Gail might say. But Richard
knew what Gail did not: Dewey was a roughshod gem.

Richard said, "Just wondered if you wanted to come back and
work."

"I got another job."

"Ah. Well, good. Good for you. Where?"

"It's decent."

Richard looked out over the trailer, Dewey looked out toward the
road, a perfect silence in the dryness of the day. Finally, too eagerly,
Richard said, "Got any beer?"

Dewey shook his head. "No way. You?"

Richard just shook his head. He made a decision, said, "Naw. But
let's go get us some." Screw it: "And we can do us up some whiskey,
too."

Dewey said nothing, but went back into his trailer for a long
minute. When he returned, the two men walked in silence back to
Richard's. Gail had left. Good. They climbed in the new minivan.

Dewey didn't want to go to the store in town, insisted they go all the way out to the general store in Leslie, a twenty-mile drive.

"Why not?" Richard said. He'd never stopped in Leslie, a one-store town up past the lakes.

To the Leslie store in silence. And in silence Richard and Dewey stood in front of the shelves of liquor, Richard feeling the money in his pocket, knowing he'd be the one to have to pay. Dewey picked out a *half gallon* of expensive whiskey, the most expensive they had, then motioned for Richard to pick his own. So Richard did, adding the prices in his head, shrugging it off: sixty bucks, so what? They walked to the counter, waited behind another customer, a woman who had a hundred questions about birdseed. Dewey nudged Richard, nodded subtly, meaningfully. Richard nodded back, as if he knew the meaning in that nod. When the counter person bent to find the price list for sunflower seed, Dewey leapt at the door, burst outside, ran to the van carrying his whiskey. The woman at the counter stood up and looked after him, looked quizzically at Richard. He paused, felt the money in his pocket, said, "Uhm . . ."

Then he jumped, too—burst out the door, into the hot sun, ran across the pavement. Behind him he heard the woman say, "Hey!" and that was all. She didn't even run after them. Probably she was calling the cops.

Dewey had taken the driver's seat so Richard had to adjust his flight at the last second and hop in the passenger side of his own little van. He flung Dewey the keys, and fast enough that no one could have gotten a good look they were out of there in a blasting cloud of front-wheel-drive dust and gravel, out of there and flying down Route 2 faster than Richard had ever dared drive. Somewhere before New Sharon, Dewey fishtailed off the highway and into the mouth of a dirt road and they bounced in the ruts to the woods.

"Jesus," Richard said.

Dewey said, "Never pay for a drink." He slowed down on the awful road. At a bend in the Sandy River, far from the main road, far from any house, high up on a bluff over mild rapids, Dewey parked. He opened his bottle and drank.

Richard's breathing slowed gradually. He opened his own bottle, hefted it to his lips. The whiskey turned him hot. Careful not to smile, he said, "That was a blast."

They watched the river.

"'A blast,'" Dewey said, mocking him. Then he was quiet. After several good slugs from his huge bottle he said, "I think you got the nuts for a real job?"

Richard knew what Dewey meant. He straightened and used his own voice, an architect's voice: "The nuts? I would say, yes. The desire, no."

"Same thing," Dewey said.

"Shit, Dew. Forget it."

"I have this idea."

"Dew, forget it."

They drank from the ungainly bottles and watched the river and hardly said anything at all. Before long Richard found himself unable to prevent a smile, kept grinning and laughing and patting his bottle of booze. "I'm as happy as I've been in years," he said.

Dewey seemed barely to hear him.

⟩ ⟩ ⟩

Because Richard had wondered aloud whether Dewey was married, big Jim called him Wedding Bells. Soon this was shortened to Bells, which seemed to stick. Happily, huge Jim was in the back of the minivan during the hour's ride to Little Henry's in Port Lawrence. Back there all his jabs and jibes and nervous patter seemed contained.

Little Henry's was a rural convenience store, and Dewey had learned somehow that on Sundays the owner was "clown" enough to keep all the money from the whole busy tourist weekend in a little safe in back—as much as $10,000 (which to Richard didn't sound like as grand a sum as it clearly did to Dewey and Jim)—such a little safe that Dewey knew Jim could lift it and carry it. Jim had been carrying rocks around for weeks—rocks twice the weight of the safe—and was ready.

Richard was to be the driver. Late nights he found it shocking that he'd agreed to this. But the plan and his place within it had fallen together incrementally, ineluctably. Richard had drunk with the boys and enjoyed the conversations—been part of the conspiracy. He honestly thought it was just talk, Sherwood Forest kind of stuff, thought nothing was ever going to come of it, thought Jim was putting enormous rocks in the van as a kind of conceptual exercise, nothing more. Yet, there was a precise night Richard had said yes. A precise night he'd taken Dewey's hand and shaken it a long damn time and said yes right in Dewey's dark eyes. Dewey's logic had been unassailable: young Baker was back in jail (he'd punched his piggish parole officer in the neck), and the gang needed a driver; Richard's minivan was perfect (wood paneling even, cute like something you'd drive nuns in); Richard (here Dewey's voice dropped solemnly) was by now part of the gang, and it was like the Marines, or the muskefuckingteers: all for one, one for all.

So Richard had clasped Dewey's hand, said yes. The very next morning, pleading at Dewey's door, Richard tried to make it no. But Dewey put an arm around Richard's neck and dragged him roughly into the trailer's kitchen, pulled a big carving knife out of a broken drawer, poked the point into Richard's forehead, drawing blood, touching skull. He said: "You gonna quit?" After a very long pause Dewey let go, put the knife away, said he was kidding, said, "Go ahead, Third Eye. Quit if you want."

Richard hadn't quit, so really he'd said yes twice. By day, the decision left him exhilarated. Nights, he slept poorly, wanted to wake Gail, desperately wanted to shake Gail from her overworked exhaustion and slumber and confess all. By day, he watched her drive off to meetings and laughed at himself: if he ever woke her she would only say he was a dope and too idle, turn back to sleep and in the morning drive off to her meetings just the same. At night he thought of Dewey's woman, thought of Dewey's kid, thought of his own kids, planned how he'd back out of this thing, how he'd tell Gail, then Dewey, how easy that would really be.

But by day he did the research required of him: the exact mileage from Little Henry's to the State Police barracks, the exact mileage to the Port Lawrence Police Department, the exact mileage to the Ledyard County sheriff's office, the exact distance on Route 2 from Little Henry's to home, the exact distance on the circuitous Route 121, the distance to all of twelve different logging roads they might disappear on, the distance to two gravel pits and a quarry in which they might hide if (Dewey's grave concern) "the pigs went bullshit."

Oh, Richard liked the excitement, liked having such a fine secret from Gail. He liked his acceptance by folks who had never noticed him at all. He liked how his wardrobe had changed (black T-shirts, a big black belt, heavy boots). He liked the way he'd stopped fitting in at Gail's many luncheons and dinners, liked how easy it was to skip them. And he loved his afternoons at Dewey's: the camaraderie, the hilarity, the feeling these guys would take care of him.

They'd all been to Little Henry's twice now, knew where the safe was (behind a white door that said EMPLOYEES ONLY and hard against a grimy toilet that the clerk had let Richard use); knew that Sunday night the kid at the counter (named Pete) would be alone; knew that the nearest police station (actually the Port Lawrence Town Office) was nearly eleven miles from the store; knew that the Sunday night police shift was the lightest of the week (one cop, who hung out in the station with the lady dispatcher, drinking coffee); knew that the much more professional state police tended to stay toward the coast and the interstate. The gang made a bunch of contingency plans, even practiced a couple of routes home, worked their way to the night they'd picked: July 23.

A hot night. Richard drove, wishing fervently that he'd said no when no was still possible. Dewey and Jim insisted on displaying their big handguns in the car. Saints wouldn't need guns. They buffed them up, stared at them, called them maggies and bones. What the hell had he been thinking? Baker, languishing in prison, had donated his firepower to the cause in exchange for a 10 percent cut. Richard had opted not to go lumpy, as the boys put it, not to carry a gun, because he couldn't use one if he had one, and had no intention of shooting or threatening anyone, no intention of getting out of the car, for that matter. He would sit there in jacket and tie, as planned, and earn his 30 percent quietly.

So in the parking lot at Little Henry's, the night dark, Richard waited. He watched the mirrors, but no one else drove in. Dead night. Almost quitting time. He saw Dewey through the big store window, Dewey rummaging through the potato chips. He couldn't see Jim. He couldn't see the clerk, either, which was the idea: if he couldn't see the clerk, the clerk couldn't see him, couldn't see the vehicle for an I.D. It had been Richard's idea, in fact, to smear mud on the license plates. No one in the mirrors.

Richard needed something for his stomach, needed to crap, needed something to eat, needed the next fifteen minutes to be over fast. He saw Dewey step to the counter with a bag of popcorn. He saw big Jim step up, too, saw Dewey yank the gun from his pants, saw Jim do the same from his, big guns in their hands, now Dewey yelling something Richard could almost hear. They waved the guns and shook them, fingers on the triggers. Richard moaned with fear.

No one in the mirror. Gail in the den at home, furious with him for going drinking again. Dewey leaning over the counter, handfuls of bills and checks and food stamps, looking mean, saying something. The kid clerk must be lying down now, as per their plan. Jim out of the picture, gone to get the safe. In the mirror, nothing. Richard remembered his job, leaned across the armrest into the back of the van, slid the side door open so the van would be ready to accept the safe. Dewey stuffing his pockets with cash. No sign of Jim. Still, cop car, entering the lot slowly, no flashing lights, no siren.

Richard thought about honking the horn, realized that might seem suspicious. He got out of the van, oddly calm, walked into the store, announced it: "Cops."

Jim was just coming out of the bathroom backwards, carrying the safe an inch off the floor. Clearly it was heavier than the rocks he'd been practicing with.

"Cops," Richard said again, louder. He stood like a customer at the counter, looked casually out. Two policemen—Staties, as Dewey called them—big men, one of them smiling, finishing some joke as he climbed out of the car.

Dewey said, "Go behind. Like you work here." He ducked down in one of the small aisles.

Richard stepped behind the counter. The clerk lay in old receipts with his face to the linoleum, panting. Jim left the safe in the middle of the floor, hopped back into the bathroom.

The cop came in.

"Hello," Richard said.

"New guy," the cop said, perfectly jocular. "What'd they? Fire Pete?"

The kid on the floor said, "Here!" Said, "Robbing! Guns!"

The cop didn't even have time to look confused or respond before Dewey stood and blasted at him. The shot was bad, smashed the big store window. The second shot was better, seemed to catch the Statie's shoulder. The gun was loud in that little place, louder than the practice shots.

"Jesus!" Richard cried.

The cop wheeled and fell to the floor and scurried forward, pushing the door open. His partner was quick, was on the radio, was out of the car, and both of them were behind it with guns drawn before Jim got out of the bathroom. He'd missed what happened, maybe thought Dewey had gotten it, ran to the door with his gun waving, opened the door even as he saw the situation, took several bullets in his chest, and fell. The kid on the floor at Richard's feet—Pete—flinched but didn't try to move.

Dewey peeked over the tampons, said, "Get over here, Bells."

But Richard couldn't.

Dewey waved the gun: "Get your shit-dick over here!"

Richard put his hands in the air so the cops would see he was unarmed, stepped from behind the counter. Dewey leapt behind him, put the gun to his neck, and said, "Go to the door."

The cops were out there holding their huge guns, scared, trying to peer into the store.

Richard had to step in Jim's blood to make the door, could hear something gurgling in Jim's big body.

"Out," Dewey said.

Richard pushed the glass door open with his belly, gun at his neck, hands in the air. "I'm an architect," he called. "I'm an architect."

"I'll shoot him," Dewey said.

"Put it down," one cop said.

"Put yours down," Dewey said. "Yours, or I shoot the architect."

Richard could see the cops weren't going to shoot, saw how young they were. Dewey led him around the van. They climbed in through the open side door, Dewey firmly pressing the gun to Richard's temple.

"Go," Dewey said, once Richard was in the driver's seat. The cops looked helpless. The one who'd been shot slumped against the cruiser, a hand pressed to his bleeding shoulder.

Richard backed up slowly into the dark street, backed up so that Dewey was never exposed. The cops didn't move till he put the van in drive and pulled out, then he saw them tumble into their car. Dewey said, "Fuck." Money stuck out of his jacket pockets.

Richard said, "Jim . . ."

"'I'm an architect,'" Dewey said. He climbed in back, opened the sliding door and when the cops were far enough out of the parking lot to see, he leapt from the van and rolled onto someone's lawn. Richard had a glimpse of him rising and running, kept driving. The cruiser's lights began to flash; in seconds the cops were close behind. Richard put his hand out the window to show that it was he, the architect, and slowly pulled to a stop in front of a farmhouse.

He climbed from the car, hands in the air, stepped toward the cops. They climbed out both sides of their car, aimed their guns at Richard's beautiful new minivan.

"He jumped out," Richard said. "He's gone."

"Get over here," the uninjured cop said.

Richard kept his hands up, made a couple of more steps.

"He's gone?" the cop said.

"Jumped out," Richard said, then lied: "He ran into the woods back there."

"You're a lucky man," the shot cop said.

"Hostage is free," the other cop said, into the radio.

⟩ ⟩ ⟩

Dewey was caught two months later trying to cash one of the checks from Little Henry's, caught on the very day that Richard passed his architecture exams. In court, just before Christmas, Dewey never looked at Richard once, never said a word to implicate him, confirmed Richard's story, the story Dewey must have read in the newspaper or seen Richard give on TV: two thugs, one of them an acquaintance, had commandeered Richard's van right in his driveway and made him take them to Port Lawrence at gunpoint. It was a pretty good story, and no one but Gail ever questioned it: she knew Richard had planned some kind of outing with those drunken fools that night, but even she would never begin to suspect the whole truth, just thought some drinking game had gotten out of hand.

Richard didn't sleep a full night till spring, waited for the lady at the Leslie General Store to come forward, waited for that kid Pete to remember that it was Richard who'd announced the cops, but the store lady never peeped, and Pete in court had called Richard brave, a hero.

> 〉 〉

Dewey is serving forty years. Jim is dead. Richard the hero mows Dewey's yard when he can, and he talks to Dewey's woman (who's not saying what she knows about that night): she's got an okay job now at the turning mill in Wilton. And Richard helps her with her many chores, takes the little boy out fishing, pays a bill or two quietly, and thinks she's begun to regard him without suspicion. She's even agreed to let him add a porch for her (it's a design he'd like to try out, he says; it's just a prototype; of course it's free), agreed to let him clear the lot of car parts and dogshit and glass. He tells her he owes her—he owes Dewey—and it's on those terms she allows him in.

Tuughannock Falls

To fly anywhere at a moment's notice is my job, very nearly. At Merrymount Hospice, the morning after the afternoon of Japonica's call ("Stephen has been asking for you"), I have to fill out a form explaining my relationship to the patient. I write, *Friends from birth.* This relationship occasions no questions, and I'm given a wristband. *Visitor.* Red letters. In the plane I've whipped my hurt and resentment into a froth, but here on the quiet walkways of this elegant factory of mental health I'm calm again, if worried: apparently Stephen has neither spoken nor otherwise communicated for two full weeks, not a peep since June 1, not until yesterday, when he began repeating my name. Which is simple: Bob Smith.

> > >

Japonica hates Bob Smith. This true fact once amused me, brought jokes to my lips, and while the jokes still fight to come, I guess I know more about me now, more of jealousy, and more what a loud and lousy influence I may have been on Stephen, and maybe just the faintest little bit about which of my qualities would have made Stephen so willing to abandon me. He hasn't spoken to anyone at all these two weeks, but he hasn't spoken to me for twenty years.

Japonica (once Janet—but I'll repress the satire): Japonica worked against me with Stephen, worked hard since the very day of the big party in Santa Barbara that saw my glorious best friend wed, but which she (and so he) wouldn't call a wedding. And I was best man, but not called best man, that phrase never used. But I accompanied the male-human-about-to-get-lawfully-attached through the days and events and pressures preceding the ceremony, and stood beside him while he made his promises in front of a room full of people seated on two sides of an aisle. A person who was not a religious figure—a ship's captain, I believe—said the twenty legal words of the rite, and the two of them, Stephen and Japonica, exchanged golden rings and read their invented vows. And we who had watched ate fish under white tents, then showered the frowning results of the day's work with birdseed, showered them and laughed and screamed till they were safe in a long white California limousine, just a car, really, just a tremendously long car that one wondered what movie star must have sat in, and what ex-president.

⟩ ⟩ ⟩

In Stephen's "pod" at Merrymount, I find the "pod station," and the "pod nurse" is lovely and gentle and not too young and smiles at me sweetly, with a quick eye to my red visitor's bracelet. "You're an old friend of Mr. Massuau's."

"The oldest."

"He's in the Santa Cruz space, just there."

And she glides around the desk on a cushion of air and glides beside me past the many potted plants and couches and low marble tables with magazines and through the perfect silence into Stephen's "space" (she can't say room, or even podlet), which is costing Mc-Donnell-Douglas Aerospace plenty, at a guess. It's a hotel room, this "space," not even a heart monitor in sight, chromium and leather furnishings, million-dollar view through high glass out to the Pacific, only the hospital bed to give it away. Stephen is still as the air in there, seated (good posture) in an expensive modular chair not quite facing the window.

"Stephen," I say gently. I'm washed in emotion; it's all I can do to stand upright and breathe.

The pod nurse floats away.

"Long time," I say, trying a couple of steps around him to look in his blank face. He looks just fine to my untrained eye, fit and tanned and only a little gray at the temples, nicely shaven, brave and trim, athletic as ever, ready to spring, hale and handsome, all fine except brown eyes aimed a little high and just to the right of the window. He doesn't move, not a blink or twitch or breath, and he doesn't gain any expression at all, just sits pleasant and expectant, a little remote, like someone waiting for good news.

"Twenty years," I say.

He just keeps waiting.

"Stephen, twenty years."

And waits.

So I give him, or what passes for him, a speech, as follows, quoting as many of our old jokes as possible, hearing their misfirings even as I speak, using our old high-goof diction, seeing myself as Japonica must have all these years, that is: negatively, inescapably negative, all my organs sinking in the cavity of my chest, pressing on my guts. And through this speech, anger rises.

I say, "I missed you, brother. You move out to the land where plastic plants grow wild, and never again do I hear from you. Oh, I know you must have wanted to stay in touch. I know this, and I know that Janet's to blame—Japonica, I mean, sorry, sorry—but twenty years, Stephen? You deserve some of the blame, too, rocket boy. I hear about your kids from Billy O'Rourke, I hear about your big promotions from the fucking *Wall Street Journal*. I send congrats. I send stuffed toys. I send a check for sweet sixteen to Miranda, a pretty name, your daughter, Stephen, a pretty young woman, no doubt. I send birth announcements for my kids you've never met and never a note back from you, Stephen. And I know what it is. It's her. What'd I ever do to her? At worst, what? Maybe put her down to you and occasionally made fun of her to you, and okay: impugned her, indicted her, maligned her, denounced her, spoofed her? Twenty years back, though. I was just jealous, I was, I understand that now, I see that about myself now. I was jealous and felt abandoned, I suppose the therapists would say. In fact, I had a therapist and that's what she said, exactly. And I talked about you pretty much the whole three sessions. Yes, only three because it was all just talk (also, I had a dream wherein the word *therapist* was broken in two: *the rapist*). And the talk did make me realize what a hole you left. Oh, Stephen. You look great. You look just great to me sitting here. You look like the last time I clapped eyes on you. Not a day older. But Stephen, come on, no note, nothing when Linda passed away? Nothing when my wife you never met died? I didn't send you a *note*, was that it? I know my father did send you a note, a quiet tasteful note, and not a word from you. But all that's forgiven. All that. Twenty years. Was my contempt at the surface of those letters I wrote? Did I brag too much, trying to impress you? Was I nothing to you? Did you ever even think of me?"

Long pause. He's impassive. The stillness invites calm. I settle down, change gears, give him news: "My girls have a car each now. Can you imagine our folks buying us cars at that age? Not a chance. And Sarah is gay, she thinks. Can you imagine a parent copping to that when we were kids? She has a partner who's big as me, and tougher and I let them sleep in her room together. What the hell, right? It's their lives, and I like having smart women around. I told them your joke from college: *What's the difference between a whale and an Ithaca lesbian?* Fifty pounds and a flannel shirt. Is the punch line. Now they want to go to Cornell. And with her grades and her girlfriend's connections they'll get in."

〉 〉 〉

Where the newlycommitteds went after the ceremony, I can't quite remember—never heard details. Because that was it, that hug be tween Stephen and me just before the clunky ceremony in the little side room at the mansion Japonica's chilly folks rented for the nuptials (I believe is a fair word). That hug lasted so long that the synthesizer player had to come back and ask us to come on out and join the party, unless we weren't invited, ho ho. She was a funny one, that little synthesizer player, and played the Wedding March despite being instructed, even commanded, not to by Stephen's new legal life partner.

〉 〉 〉

Not a movement from my old friend. Not a blink of the eye, not a nod of the head, not a tear on the cheek, not a tap of the foot, not a twitch of the lip. He looks *tremendous*—healthy and wise, clean and brave, courteous and kind. The room is sparkling, pinks and ivories; the curtains billow with sweet Pacific wind. I keep talking. His presence is so human and electrical somehow that I start to believe he is listening. I go on and on, interrogating the past, trying to build something firm, a temple of friendship in which we might meet.

I fire questions: "Did we hike in the forests, you and I? Did we drink in the bars? Did we study till morning, side by side? Did we eat LSD and stare at snow banks? Did we sleep with brilliant women, sometimes the same one? Did we wrestle and grapple and fistfight and hug? Did we eat methamphetamines on long drives and talk nonstop and confess our beautiful Platonic love for one another? Did people not refer to us as Steve and Bob? Or Bob and Steve? Were we not closer than twin suns bound by gravity eternally (or at least till supernova did us part)?

"Did we not finish college and finish well despite all? Did I not move to California with you when the time came for graduate school? Did you not make fun of me for taking yoga classes? Did I chastise you for seeking and finding high-end work in the Military Industrial Complex? Did we handle this, too, and all things? Was it not I who introduced you to Janet from yoga class? Yoga class, Stevie! We used to shout with laughter, you making fun of me for yoga. But I found you a girl, I did."

Not a twitch.

"You are my friend," I say. "Twenty years cannot change that." I get up and look out the window. This is too painful. Far below us the ocean is rough and roiling, one surfer out there paddling around, no wave to catch. But the breeze is strong, rattles the stout jade plants outside the podlet window. I live in Virginia, for lovers. I work in Washington, D.C., for lawyers. There is no ocean upon which to gaze in those precincts. I'm a lobbyist for anyone who will hire me, except Tobacco, War, Gross Polluter, Fundamentalist. Which leaves almost nothing.

"You little fuck," Stephen says distinctly.

But I'm staring out the window at the ocean. When I look back Stephen's as still as before. I'm not hearing things, I know; I never hear things, I know a voice when I hear it, and I know Stevie's fond voice, too, the voice of old.

"Stephen?"

His face is composed and fresh and just the same as when I first walked in, but for a stronger smile.

"I see you grinning," I say.

And the grin grows and the eyes flash with fire and he rocks in his chair, all youthful energy, and says, "Get me out of here!" And he's giggling, tittering, trying to hold it back, snorting, spitting. He manages a stage whisper: "Jesus, Bobbo, what happened to me?"

I sputter. It's all a joke: "You were, uh, catatonic for a few weeks there." And we just roar like little boys, like when together we went to his synagogue and he couldn't control himself at the sight of goyim me in a *yarmulke*: junior high school.

"Sounds *great*," he says. And he's up on his feet—no stopping him, looking at his clothes, looking at me. And looking at me, he's taken aback. Our laughter just dies. "How long've I been *out*?" he says. "You look *fifty years old*, you fucker!"

"I'm forty-five," I say soberly.

"Rip Van fucking Winkle," he says, examining me closely, as if to understand my disguise. "Political satire. A critique of the new vulgar America." He's quoting something wryly verbatim from our sophomore English class, something a middle-aged engineer ought to have forgotten. Then, "Two minutes ago you're passing me a bong of red Leb, turn around and you're *fat* and you're *gray*." He is making fun of me in his oldest style, but at the same time he's shocked by my appearance, trying unsuccessfully to hide dismay with laughter. He's one of these never-let-'em-see-you-sweat guys, and he's always been damn good at it: *Your friends are suddenly middle-aged? No problem.*

"I'm not so goddamn fat," I tell him.

He leaps to his feet, limps around the room clowning to hide any panic, gets in front of the mirror, examines himself, clutches his thighs in real pain, slumps to the floor, loose as a college kid. "Okay," he says seriously. "What happened?"

"Well, you seem to be missing a few years, Stephen. Probably it'll all come back to you. Japonica and your daughter and McDonnell-Douglas Aerospace, the works."

"Accident?"

"You just went blank, apparently."

"Japonica?"

"You know: *Janet*?"

Nothing.

"She is your wife."

He takes this news calmly, looks at me a long time. He's going to make do with what he's got. He says, "Last I remember is you at Taughannock. Oh! That fucking shale! You had my wrist, right? Oh, shit, oh my God, that fucking shale! I fucking *fell*!" He's terrified suddenly, feels his head where the brutal split was twenty-five years back, but there's no split there now. He fell, all right, fell in a shower of shale ledge that no one smart would have climbed ever, not to 200 feet. But we did, having argued its safety, me on the side of climbing, I regret to say. Bounced all the way down to the creek, he did. Split his scalp, cracked the skull, bathed himself in blood, head to foot. Broke both *thighs*, his two femurs, the heaviest bones in the human body. To hear the cries that preceded the silence! To climb down in the growing dusk! To have to leave him to climb back out and sprint for help!

"I'll get a nurse," I say.

"No way," he says. "Get a wheelchair. No one'll think twice. We're *out of here*."

Word for word and tone for tone, this is precisely what he said in the neurological unit at Tompkins County Hospital when we were twenty. I mean exactly, and with the exact look in his eye, and the same hand on his head, only now there is no shaved skull, no bandage. At that age and all those years ago I was game, baby, and I wheeled him out to my disintegrating station wagon and off to the Falls to show him where he fell, and to spend the night with him in the woods there by a big fire with two girls, one named Chrissy Miles, one forgotten. Next day the doctors didn't think it was funny, but they released him. His folks, they never forgave me.

"Well, we better not do that," I say. "I'll go get that pod nurse."

"Is she *sexy*?" Stephen says. He's twenty. He says, "God, I haven't gotten laid in *weeks*."

"She's sexy," I say. I haven't gotten laid in longer than weeks, is what I'm thinking, till death do you part notwithstanding.

"Get me out of here," Stephen says, and we can't help it, we laugh and laugh and laugh and laugh. And laugh.

⟩ ⟩ ⟩

Japonica is civil with me, and I'm careful not to call her Janet. She doesn't invite me over to their canyon home, nothing like that, but the two of us meet in the Main Pod Lobby of Merrypod, which is very comfortable, like a hotel bar without the bar, leather club chairs and many plants, sun from the skylights high above.

She's still good-looking, still with the slight cast in her eye, but now she's behind giant designer eyeglasses. She's tall as ever, but thinner than I recall, which was too thin always. Her lips are puffed unnaturally and her mouth, really, it's gorgeous, oh my, still gorgeous. I can picture her in a bikini and also topless on Muir Beach all those years ago and also naked in my bed (baby talk) and in hers, two weeks of good fun. I can remember her laughing with me after yoga class, cruel laugh. I can remember introducing her to Steve at the beach party I brought her to. And I remember the mechanism by which my hot and hopeful fling became Steve's girlfriend over the next several days: *We're just not right together.* Stevie missing at night for weeks, nothing said till my old girl Jill turned up for an extended stay, then love in the open, Stevie and Janet, a thin wall away.

My jealousy, my God, it was like horses inside me, horses reined to the very posts of my heart, their snorting breath escaping my mouth snidely, restrained fury writing my joky, mean script, my lips smiling, always smiling, never saying the central thing. Jill said I'd changed, and then she left me, too.

"Remember that little minuscule Yogi?" I bark.

"Can a person be both little and minuscule at once?" Japonica answers, not kidding.

"I used to sit behind you in that class to smell your perfume," I say.

"I cannot handle any more of these tests they're putting him through," she says. But her gaze has flickered: she loved me briefly.

"And that's how you and Steve met," I say.

"Oh, Bobby, one minute he was fine, the next minute he was sitting stock-still out by the pool with the phone still in his hand. And poor Miranda thought, Well, he's joking! And she's out there laughing at him! Giving him tickles! Poor child. She's devastated. Blames herself, irrationally."

"It's that little smile. That makes it seem like he's kidding."

"He asked for you," she says for the tenth time in ten conversations, in a tone as if to say I should agree that this request of his was preposterous and a sure sign of worse affliction than any of us want to imagine.

"He thinks he's back in Ithaca," I say for the tenth time in ten conversations. Then add fresh material: "He wants to escape from the hospital like we did back then. He wants a bong hit. You know, that kind of thing."

"You two were such thorough reprobates."

"We were very close, Japonica."

"Dr. Smolkins doesn't buy your theory."

Which is that Stephen's old injury has come back, is all, and somehow the brain damage from back then has suddenly decided to erase everything that happened since. Smolkins says it's a stroke, which he calls an episode—but he hasn't actually denounced my theory, not at all. That's an exaggeration. He's only cautious about it.

Japonica sighs mightily, looks at me accusingly. "Stephen doesn't remember me at all," she says.

"That must hurt," I tell her softly.

〉 〉 〉

Dr. Smolkins is not sure at all what to do with Stephen, who is awake now, and very polite with everyone who comes to visit, but doesn't remember them, not a glimmer. I come every afternoon, just after five, so as to briefly see Japonica, who must fetch their daughter up from field hockey practice daily.

Stephen says, "I can't believe I married that chick. She's like my mother. She's a *bitch*. She's awful. And she hates you. What did you do to her, fucker?"

"She was a great beauty," I say.

"No one is that great a beauty."

"I brought a little something," I say. And present the pink shopping bag from the Sunshine Daydream store in the Escondito Mall. Ceremoniously, I pull out the bong. There's no weed to go with it, of course, though Dr. Smolkins says there's no defect that would prevent our man from living a normal life. He might possibly go home as soon as Tuesday, if the last test comes out as the good doctor predicts. But home is where the heart is, and Stevie's heart is with me for the moment. Or me at age twenty, at any rate.

"And my daughter, shit, my *daughter*, Bob. She is—*hot*! My God. She must have friends, right? I mean, I can't touch her, right? Even though I don't know her?"

His daughter is pretty, all right, pierced belly button and tall heels. I've only glimpsed her, older high-school girl. We must forgive him. Stephen is to relearn not only his life, but years of gained maturity. That's the plan. He's to go in there and play the role till he grows back into it. Twenty-five years he'll have to age. Aeronautical engineering he'll have to restudy, though Smolkins says it may all come back at any time. And he'll have to walk a little better, too. His legs are weak for no reason Smolkins can figure, but I know what it is: twin fractured femurs. Our boy Stevie hobbled around for months after, limped for years. I recognize the hobble, I tell Smolkins, but Smolkins has got his cues from Janet, and just closes his ears to me, shakes his head.

〉 〉 〉

Japonica's call was a sudden rip in the healing fabric of my life. Not a word from her in twenty years, not a word from Stephen for seventeen (and that word a Christmas card picturing their new daughter). I stayed big as I could, called a lot and wrote and later faxed and later still e-mailed, and even in mourning begged a little: just a word, just a nod. I even told them as I grew older and more able to confess my feelings that I was hurt. And further, apologized for anything I might have done. But nothing.

In fact, this tough and wily Washington lobbyist, myself, began to weep the second Japonica said her name. I wept and moaned and carried on, all my losses mounting.

She said, "Stephen is asking for you."

〉 〉 〉

Stevie-boy rolls the bong in his hands critically, a budding engineer, not even a B.A. left in his head: "This is drilled all wrong, the carburetor invection is reversed." And inspects it some more, suddenly agitated. He looks at me in undisguised undergraduate panic: "Bobbo, you got to get me out of here. These people are fucked. That woman? I don't want to live with her!"

That's it. I go down to the nurses' pod and greet Marylou, who is sexy indeed and moreover seems to like me. "A wheelchair?" I ask, casually. "Stephen wants a little walk."

"Oh! Wonderful!" says Marylou. My God, she's cheerful.

She goes to the storage podlet and locates us a fine little chariot. I decline her help and roll the thing down to the space named Santa Cruz. Stephen giggles when he sees me, hobbles across the room despite healthy legs, falls into the chair in a way I recall exactly, accepts the blanket across his lap, and we are off, brothers in crime. I wheel him clear to the back of the property, where there's a redwood fence of some quality. I simply and would like to say deftly kick a few boards out and crawl through and I'm in the parking lot I've been towed from twice now. Steve crawls through, too, with difficulty, as if his perfectly good, middle-aged legs are broken, then I fold the chair and pull it through. I set the fence boards more or less back in place, no one to see us, and then I wheel my best and oldest friend down the hill to my red rental car, an upgrade, still small.

And we're off, laughing and singing, trading insults, rock and roll radio, waving at girls too young by miles, stopping off for beer. My I.D. is fine, I tell Stephen, it's just fucking fine. And we laugh and laugh and laugh and laugh until the old man comes out of the store to see what's funny, and we're laughing so jollily, he laughs, too. We speed down to Muir Beach, an old haunt that Stevie cannot remember, and wheel that deluxe pod chair out on the sand and sit there in the sun drinking beers and laughing more, and harder. He's twenty and I'm twenty and he's just defied the gods and lived through the worst climbing accident his doctors have ever seen or heard of. We're good students at a great American university, and we're alive, alive, alive. And the world, weirdly, has changed little at all. Stevie punches my shoulder and I punch his and we swim naked as seals and he hobbles up onto the beach as if his legs are fresh out of casts and hot girls walking by check us out because we are twenty and we are full of the universe and roaring with fun and we are beautiful, full of possibility.

When the massive cerebral hemorrhage kills him he has just punched my shoulder again, and called me Bobbo, and the waves are rolling in, and Japonica may forgive me yet, as Smolkins does, based on that last test he did: Stevie's brain was a time bomb, it was. And I, well, I just count myself lucky to have been back in his heart when the big bang came, and to know there are more hearts to win.

Fredonia

George Skinner drives to Michigan every six weeks for the store, and every six weeks he drives right past Fredonia, New York, where his sister lives with her husband Kevin. He doesn't stop. Every six weeks he thinks about brilliant Tracy Lynn, thinks about how he ought to stop this time, how he is going to stop this time, thinks about it from the toll booth at Nyack until just past the exit near Fredonia, and then he changes the subject in his mind, drives an hour more to a familiar and thoroughly crummy motel. He prefers not to drive straight through.

Tracy Lynn. He has her number written on the little emergency card that came with his wallet, so if anything bad happens to him she'll be the first to hear. Twice in the past year he's gotten off at the exit and rumbled through Fredonia and looked at the SUNY campus and thought about her teaching there. Once he went so far as to park the truck at a pair of meters and walk around and ask where the Philosophy Department might be, had a look at the handsome building from afar, then fed himself a slow dinner at a place she might go, a health food place, brown rice with some kind of sesame stuff, not the worst thing he ever ate, but she didn't turn up, and he drove on.

In Ann Arbor he stays at the Sheraton and eats well and drinks a little with Carl Gerhardt, and they talk furniture, old furniture, the antiques Carl's collected in six weeks, or they talk people, the people Carl has bought from and bargained with and cheated, really, and swindled. George Skinner has begun to know a little bit about antiques thanks to Carl, who claims to be a world-class expert. They have never had a private conversation, yet this time George opens his mouth after two scotches in the hotel bar and says, "I'm going to stop and see my sister on the way back. She's in Fredonia, right off the highway, and you know, I've never stopped in."

And Carl says, "There's a barn back there, it's just below Fredonia, almost down to Chautauqua, a delicious old place; well, it used to be delicious. New owner—the party, Georgie boy, is over—but at one time the old couple there would sell you an original Shaker table like it was a card table, something a bit plain but useful, just useful, you know. Morons! Look for it, it's a big old barn, used to be in poor repair—the new guy's got it painted. He is sharp, sharp, sharp—too bad for us. Right on Route 60, just past Cassadaga, shitbelly town. Bright yellow barn. It's not the same, but it's worth a look."

"I haven't even talked to her."

Carl looks a little surprised, raises up his eyebrows. He is bald and the shining top of his head is always very white from wearing a beret, of all things, in the sun. He looks like some kind of duck hunter, red-and-white-checked woolen jacket, flannel shirt, like that, except for this beret, which makes him look exactly like someone who knows everything about every piece of furniture ever made or bought by a farmer in the history of the Midwest. "Who?" he says.

"My sister, Tracy Lynn. She's in Fredonia. I'm going to see her on the way back."

"They've gotten very smart back there. Well, smart everywhere. Now they want a thousand for some shop project a generation old. Morons."

"She's thirty-seven."

"Old enough to by-God know better."

Carl and George are both forty this year.

"We'll get some college kids," Carl says. He means college kids to unload his truck and reload George's. "See you in the morning." And that's it; Carl picks up his beret and spins it on his finger twice, as always, and puts it on, looking humorlessly in the mirror behind the bottles. "Night." And he heads out of the bar. He's portly but manages a saunter, saunters out of the bar and stands in front of the elevator in his beret. George wonders at the beret every time. It's the perfect affectation.

And orders another drink, unusual for him—it's eleven o'clock for Christ's sake—spends an hour thinking how he's going to call. Plans the call. He doesn't foresee a problem in calling. Hi, Tracy Lynn, he thinks, it's George. I'll be coming through Fredonia today and thought I'd stop and say hello. Or: I thought I'd stop and drop off a little something I got for you all. A wedding present finally! Or: Hi, Tracy Lynn, it's George. Mom asked me to call. That would be a joke from the old days. His mother is in poor health and she doesn't ask him anything anymore when he goes to see her up there in the Odd Fellows home in Peekskill, close to him, far from Tracy. Or: Hi, Kevin! Tracy Lynn there? What do you mean, "Who's this?" Who're you? That's the question. Who the fuck are you, professor? *Moron.* Give me Tracy. I want to talk!

Five or six other people meditate solemnly over their drinks at the bar, but the happy young woman who is the bartender closes up anyway at midnight. George walks to the elevator and stands there. He smiles thinking of Carl in that ridiculous beret, puts his sister out of his mind, keeps waiting for the elevator. After a long five minutes the bartender walks by on her way to the kitchen with a tray full of glasses, including his. She seems friendly and soft looking, George thinks, like most people who don't live in New York City, and smiles at him as he waits there, actually reaches out as she passes and pats him on the shoulder, an astonishing gesture.

"I'm all right," he says.

She just shrugs and smiles like a nurse and keeps walking to the kitchen with her clinking tray. George waits some more, patiently enough, then remembers to push the button.

⟩ ⟩ ⟩

George Skinner would be embarrassed to walk up to strangers, these college kids, and ask if they want to work. Carl, however, is quite good at it. In the beret maybe he looks to them like some kind of history professor: "Hi. We need help moving some furniture. Fifty dollars for an afternoon's labor." Almost every kid stops and thinks about it, and it never takes more than twenty minutes to collect two, usually a pair of friends. Today the first one is a young man with long neat hair in a ponytail, a handsome boy, somewhat cocky, who has no trouble stopping whatever it was he was doing and standing with Carl and George, talking about furniture. His name is Eric. His mother has a dynasty table, his brother used to build furniture, his friend Arnold collects antique molding planes. George listens to Eric in small amazement: this kid at nineteen is more at ease than George himself at forty. Carl has an aloof way with the boy, knows just the degree by which to ignore him. George feels like a dumb truck driver at the periphery of the boy's attention, keeps quiet, watches him.

Carl has never asked young women to help, but Eric, joining confidently in, asks everyone gender regardless, and soon a large young woman is bargaining both Eric's and her own wage up to sixty dollars. She is athletic and confident, older than Eric, maybe a grad student, freckles and a canny smile. No one is going to take advantage of her. She argues good-naturedly about getting paid in advance; Carl argues back, less good-naturedly, and wins. She's wearing a skirt over some tight leggings or long underwear (George can't decide which and shouldn't be looking anyway, he thinks, long legs, hiking boots), so she'd like to change her clothes before she starts. They arrange to meet her at the R.C. Quad—which apparently Carl has heard of and can find—at noon. Her name is Tracy.

"That's my sister's name," George says, with more emotion than he'd like, sounding as if the young woman has stolen something valuable. It's a sweet spring day.

Carl mentions breakfast, and college-boy Eric wants to come along, which surprises George. At Eric's age George may or may not have said yes to a little work, but he knows and remembers clearly that he would never have stood around with two almost middle-aged guys and had anything to say, and knows further that he would have made any excuse to avoid sitting down to breakfast with them. But Eric comes along, even leads the way, jawboning mightily as they walk to a diner Carl is fond of for pancakes. George finds something to like about Eric as the kid gabs through the meal, though the same traits that are likeable—the confidence, the ready jokes, the desire to be admired—are also irritating. You might think the kid is a furniture major, the way he goes on. He actually knows something, more than George does. Carl wears his beret, corrects the kid from sentence to sentence. George remembers that Carl has two teenage sons back home in Nebraska.

⟩ ⟩ ⟩

At noon exactly they pull up in front of some old buildings on the campus. George fails to see anything to rightly call a quad, nothing square at all. When he mentions it, neither Carl nor the young man seems to understand his point, or that he is joking. Tracy, the grad student, is right there waiting, in blue jeans now, careful new rips across the thighs, skin showing. She has a big flannel shirt on, for work. She is tall, and looks like she'll be able to move some furniture. Carl, surprisingly, hasn't made a single grumpy comment about her. She climbs in beside him in George's truck. Eric falls silent. He seems to have used up all his furniture lore. Carl has fallen silent, too, leans forward out of the way of the two kids' wide shoulders, holds his chin, starts to fall into his bargaining funk, a mood that overtakes him at just this point at each of his and George's meetings.

It's George's job to inspect the furniture Carl has collected, and Carl dislikes George for it, even though—probably because—it's not expert things George looks for, but bad flaws: missing legs, mismatched shelves, rotten wood, worm damage, smashed glass, gouges, carvings, scratches, stains. Carl dislikes him for it because Carl is always trying to slip something by, and George generally catches it. Mr. Bergenstaedtler, George's boss, understands Carl, somehow, treats Carl's dishonesty as a foible, the flaw of a genius. George doesn't see it this way at all, sees Carl as a creep, dislikes him a little more each time he finds something wrong, each time he points out a blown seat on a rocker described in Carl's bill of lading as perfect.

They're all quiet as George drives back through the spring-green town to the Sheraton, out next to the malls on destroyed farmland in clear, sweet air. He pulls the big stick shift and pumps the hard clutch and backs the beeping Bergenstaedtler rig end-to-end and not ten feet from Carl's truck, which is moored in the far reaches of the vast and empty hotel parking lot near some luckless trees.

Carl says, "You folks go ahead and start," and marches leaning forward across the lot and into the hotel. He'll come out just when his truck's been unloaded, and having established that he isn't needed for the moving, he'll stand for the reloading and supervise.

The unloading isn't a simple matter of running furniture from one truck to the other. Carl has the heavy pieces packed at the far front of his box, and those pieces must go first into the big white

Bergenstaedtler truck. Tracy and Eric help George empty Carl's rented truck onto the blacktop of the parking lot, dig all the chairs out of the way, stand them up in the luscious breeze, open the moving mats to have a long look, checking each item off on Carl's list, noting the condition, noting whether Carl's description seems to match the piece. He's listed all the chairs as good, one or two excellent, none poor, and George accepts all of them as described. Next, as always, there are some small tables, then a couple of bedsteads, then some bookcases, then several large tables, then the really big stuff, which today is a desk and three bureaus. At the very back of the load there's a monster, all wrapped in quilted moving blankets. They begin to struggle with it just as Carl reappears.

"What's this thing?" Eric says.

"That's the bloody prize of the day," Carl says. "Let's move the oak piece first."

Tracy gets a hold on the desk. George watches her down there in the darkness of the truck, amused, expects her to need to show how strong she is, maybe lift the one side of it, maybe be impatient as Eric has been. But she's only feeling its width, getting the heft. Eric, when he joins her, lifts his end up, acting like it's not heavy as hell, picks it up a few inches, moves it toward him, has to drop it—boom!—in the resounding box of the truck body.

"Careful!" Carl barks. He's standing out in the sun, just watching. He says, "Let's back the trucks together. Stop and let's back the trucks. That's too heavy."

The kid, Eric, sighs. Tracy, though, immediately gets the picture, follows George out of the truck, stands in the parking lot just where he'll be able to see her and she can direct his short backing up. George climbs up in the cab of the Bergenstaedtler truck, starts it, lets it run a moment, watching the girl in the mirror. He's startled, suddenly notices her sexiness, this small facet of her large capability. He hasn't had a kiss or even a fond hug for something like six months, and she's a good-looking soul, strong and young and happy.

Admonishing himself, he backs the truck carefully up against Carl's, stops when Tracy signals he should, and pretty soon they're all climbing up into the gap between the two, moving into the dark, carrying the oak desk into the Bergenstaedtler truck, dropping it to one side, room to pass with the big piece that's left.

Back in Carl's truck, they stand around the monster, undraping it, looking for handholds. Carl sees there's no way he's not needed and joins them. "It's a *delicious* piece," he says. "It's a perfect piece. Go easy. It'll fetch thirty grand, at least. Wait till Bergie sees it!"

They horse it to the door of the truck and carefully, grunting with the effort, get it across the unevenly married tailgates and into the back of Bergenstaedtler's truck and rest a minute, making exclamations.

George says, "Let's uncover it so I can get a look."

"It's fine," Carl says testily.

"I want to see," Tracy says.

"It's perfect," Carl says. He puts his hands on it, ready to move it back into the darkness, but George isn't with him, and so the college kids aren't. Amazing how immediately, instinctively, they bank away from Carl's authority, side with George.

"Let's just have a look," George says. He's fighting a feeling of pointlessness. He knows from Carl's irritation that the piece has some major flaw, knows that the bill of lading is going to say *perfect*, knows that he and Carl will argue, knows that Bergenstaedtler will admire the piece despite its horrible flaws, knows the old man won't listen or care. George pulls the first mat off the monster anyway.

The kid helps out, and soon the huge hutch-like thing is exposed. Immediately Eric starts spouting about its probable age, admiring it, but George isn't listening, focusses instead on the huge, fresh gash in its side, likely some kind of forklift wound, Carl being lazy: not the first time.

George looks at him hard and says, "How did you list this?"

"It's a Turner breakfront," Carl says. "A delicious piece."

"Magnificent," Eric says, ready to adopt whatever personality is strongest around him.

"How do you list it?" George repeats.

Carl doesn't answer. The game has started.

"Let's see the list."

"I've got it down as good," Carl answers, "and that's conservative as hell. It's a real piece."

"It's gorgeous," Tracy says. "But what's this *mega* gouge? And all this here?" She points to where the finish is scraped and stripped in the most obvious place, right across the top. "I would call it a mess."

George is pleased to have an ally. Amazing how these kids can speak their minds. "I'd say fair," George says, though maybe good wouldn't be such an exaggeration. He knows that saying anything is going to get Carl going.

"What a shame," Tracy says. "Did you drop it or something?" She seems already to know the things George took so long to learn about Carl.

"It's fine," Carl says. "Bergenstaedtler's going to love it. So let's get it loaded so I can get out of here."

"Just a little refinishing," Eric says, sounding like a cocky, college-kid version of Carl.

Tracy picks up the printout, finds the breakfront: *Turner, c. 1820.* "It's listed as perfect," she says.

"No way," George says.

"Oh, Christ," Carl says, pulling his beret down off his shining head, "just load the goddamn thing, will you, George?"

George hesitates, scratches his cheek. "I don't think so, Carl." Something about the presence of the young woman has made George bold: "In fact, I think I'm going to refuse it."

"You can't refuse it."

"Consider it refused. If you can't write an honest report, then just consider it refused."

Carl slumps a little, smiles for probably the first time today, tries a good-guy approach: "You can't refuse this stuff, George."

"It's refused. Kids, let's put the breakfront back in Carl's truck."

Tracy is ready, seems excited by the argument, but Eric seems to have taken Carl's side now.

Carl climbs down off the mated tailgates, clomps away. George and Tracy are all grins, either out of fear or because Carl is so comical in his anger. Eric isn't sure what side to be on, rocks foot to foot. Suddenly, Carl's truck roars starting and lurches, pulls away, rumbles clear to the other end of the parking lot, hundreds of bleak yards of asphalt, where Carl parks it and leaps out, trots back over like someone about to throw punches. He stands below George, says, "Should I call Bergie?"

"The piece is refused."

"It's in your truck, *moron*."

"It's going to get out of my truck." George leans into the piece, and with Tracy's help slides it till it's hanging over the tailgate at the balance point, dangerously close to falling.

"You *fucking* moron," Carl says.

And Eric makes his decision. He and Tracy get on the ground, tip the Turner breakfront toward them, and within seconds it's standing on the pavement of the parking lot.

"Refused," George says.

Glowering, Carl hisses, "*You can't refuse it.*"

George picks up the bill of lading, writes REFUSED over the breakfront, shows it to Carl.

"I'm going to make a call," Carl says. "I'm going in the hotel to give Helmut Bergenstaedtler a call."

George shrugs, and Tracy shrugs with him.

Carl is red right up to the edge of his beret, making an effort not to lose his temper completely. "*Moron.*" Plain statement. He turns and marches to the grand entrance of the Sheraton, hundreds of yards the other way across the parking lot, disappears inside.

"Let's load the rest of this stuff," George says. And with the kids he pushes the biggest desk into place, then loads the bureaus, then the bookcases and tables, then all the chairs. Carl is gone a long time, and when he's back the Bergenstaedtler truck is nearly full, the rear of the load carefully tied so things won't fall. The breakfront looms alone on the pavement, just standing there. George and Tracy and Eric lean in the back of the truck in a space just about big enough for a Turner breakfront, c. 1820. They watch Carl's progress toward them. He doesn't look as if he's calmed down any.

"You can't refuse it," Carl shouts before he's fifty feet away.

"I take it Mr. B. wasn't there," George says.

"You can't refuse it, you *moron*," Carl says.

"Don't call him that," Tracy says. She's so game that George has to laugh.

Carl ignores her, stomps the pavement once in a childish gesture. "Put the fucking thing in your fucking truck, George!"

"Here you go." George hands Carl the bill of lading with the big REFUSED written on it, stuffs his own copy in his shirt pocket. Tracy jumps down from the tailgate, puts her hands about a mile deep in her pockets, the perfect gesture. Eric follows, then George jumps down, too, pulling the overhead door closed behind him. The breakfront stands naked on the pavement, forlorn.

"You can't refuse it," Carl says, trying to be nice again.

"I already have. Get your truck over here and we'll throw it in for you."

Carl says, "*Mor-on*," just that, two syllables powered with steam, then trots off across the parking lot and to his truck. He clambers in, starts it up, roars the engine a couple of times, backs up, jerks forward, but instead of coming over for the breakfront, he drives slowly to the parking lot entrance, waits for traffic, pulls out trundling, and drives away with an angry wave.

"Whoa," Eric laughs, impressed.

"He'll be back," Tracy says.

"What about the Turner breakfront?" Eric says.

There's a long silence, really long, ten minutes, the three of them just standing there in the clear air staring off the direction Carl drove. They're tired from the work. The sunlight is slanting. A flock of dusty-looking sparrows swoop into the thin branches of the moribund landscaping trees, chittering and peeping.

Finally George says, "Let's go have a drink. If he doesn't come back in an hour, I guess we'll just load it up."

⟩ ⟩ ⟩

All night George is sick with remorse. He knows he's overstepped his authority by about seven light years, knows that he has to meet up with Carl again, work with him, work with Bergenstaedtler.

Over drinks he tried to explain this to the young woman, Tracy (who as it turned out was working toward a Ph.D. in psychology, of all things), but all she could say was that he should quit if they expected him to act against his morals. He called her an idealist, and next thing he knew she was working on him, trying to ferret out the reasons for his life. She seemed surprised that he had a bachelor's degree from Columbia, which struck her as an *awesome* school, worked this small discovery into her annoying analysis. Eric just kept announcing how amazed he was about Columbia, how you never knew, how it showed you shouldn't judge people or books by their covers, callow revelations he seemed to find profound and infinitely repeatable.

After a couple of drinks and an hour of the two university kids trying to allay their excitement over the tussle by deconstructing George, they all went out in the parking lot and stared at the breakfront. The thing looked like some aggrieved British nobleman, just alone in the expanse of asphalt, the white Bergenstaedtler rig standing safely away. George shrugged, defeated, and unlatched the tall rear doors of the truck. The three of them loaded the breakfront in with much straining and groaning, much kidding around, much bold swearing.

Since Carl hadn't, George had to pay the kids, which he managed from his day money, Bergenstaedtler's anyway. Then Eric left. But here was the thing: Tracy lingered, standing there in the parking lot, and the two of them talked another hour, hands in their pockets, losing the buzz from the drinks. And at the end of this parlay Tracy announced she was going to New York next week for spring break anyway, and asked if she could have a ride. Easy as that: just blow off her classes and whatever graduate study she was up to and leave a week early.

Three in the morning and George is still lying awake, thinking of the girl. He should have said no.

❯ ❯ ❯

Tracy is there exactly at nine, exactly as planned, fed and ready, with a single small duffel bag that wouldn't hold enough socks for George. George is exhausted already, hungover. He gets behind the wheel and Tracy sits way down the long seat from him, and he's sorry he likes her so well. They smile at one another and off they go, down the highway, slowly in front of the full load, a few laughs about the breakfront and Carl, some silence as the trip begins. Then Tracy picks up on something George must have said in the bar, something he wishes he hadn't.

"Will we get to your sister's by tonight?"

George thinks a while, says, "I guess we shouldn't stop."

They are quiet a good half hour then, listening to some pop political talk on the radio, the kind of stuff George always listens to alone. Luckily, the subject is corporate greed, and George kind of agrees—the blood stays out of his face. Tracy, she's thinking about something else.

By lunch they haven't said ten words, but the ride is companionable enough. George has the idea that Tracy likes him, too, and he's trying to decide what to do about it. In the bar she'd talked the way kids will about what age people said she looked, had said she thought George didn't look any older than she, if you thought about it. She was wrong, George thinks. I look exactly forty, and she looks exactly twenty-six, and that's exactly fourteen reasons why the two of us are not going to get mixed up. Immediately he pictures his sister, realizes it's her voice saying all this, throwing all this doubt into the air. Why should a small age gap matter? Then again, who said this person wanted anything to do with him anyway at all?

George and Tracy eat lunch at a truck stop off the highway, and George notices how the waitress assumes without the least judgment that he and the girl are some kind of item.

Back in the truck, Tracy seems to get off on the three cups of coffee she's drunk, clicks the radio silent, starts in: "Why don't we stop at your sister's? You haven't seen her in how long?"

George remembers all he's told this voluble young woman, this strong, lovely woman who is suddenly his partner on the trip.

"Not that long, really."

"Do you guys talk on the phone?"

"Not that much. Some."

"Were you close when you were kids?"

"I think so."

"What kind of close?"

And George finds himself talking, talking at length, his childhood, his little sister, his struggles with girlfriends, his sister's brainy boyfriend, the death of his dad, his mother's way of being, which he'd never quite seen how curious it was—the kind of conversation you have with someone you want to see again, someone you want to date, someone you want to love and wake up with and cook for and brag about and have small jokes with and tell your day to.

"You were *injured*. That's what's wrong. That's exactly it. Your mother wounded you." Too earnestly.

"Oh, crap. Who said anything was wrong?"

"Yes, that's it exactly. You hate women, and you've set your sister up to take all the blame and you're lonely and guilty and the question is why?"

"I'm not sure I buy all this."

"You might not buy it, but you're leading a lonely life! Why?"

"I had a father, too, you know, not just a mother."

They were silent a long time, bouncing rhythmically on the joints in the pavement.

"But he's not the issue, is he . . . ?"

"No one's the issue. Why would I hate women?"

"It's just an *otherness* thing."

"Oh, come on," George says. "That's just gibberish. You've accused me of hating women—now you have to explain why."

"You tell me."

"I like women."

"All women?"

"No."

"Whom do you hate?"

"Don't you mean who?"

"It's *whom*," Tracy says. "It's a whole direct-object thing."

"I hate . . ."

"How do you get along with your mother now?"

"My mother is sick. She's eighty."

"So she was a pretty old mom, if you're forty."

"Well, yeah. She would have been my age now when I was born."

"Did she pay attention to you?"

"I don't want to be psychoanalyzed, really." He really doesn't. He looks at the radio longingly, tries a joke: "Just give me the Thorazine! Lay on the Prozac!"

But Tracy isn't going to let up—not even a smile: "This isn't analysis. And drugs are for addicts. I just want to figure out why you're so afraid of your sister."

"All this 'How do you feel about that?' crap really bugs me. I do not hate my sister. Whatever happened to the triumph of cognitive-behavioral psychology I read about in college?"

"I'm pissing you off," she says. "That's a good sign."

"I'm not pissed. You're the one that's pissed."

More silence, more bouncing down the road. A farmhouse, a bigger truck passing, grand clouds ahead and to all sides.

Tracy says, "So let's stop and see her."

More serious than he wants to sound, George says, "Maybe we should."

"Be fun!"

"How am I going to explain you?"

"We'll say I'm your therapist." Tracy holds a straight face for a second, but laughs, a surprising burble.

"Crap," George says. He likes her laugh, laughs, too.

"We'll say I'm your helper, all right?"

George just shakes his head mildly, drives.

"Which is what I am."

A long silence, twenty minutes, just the road coming, the truck bouncing.

"You are a very beautiful girl," George says, finally. "I don't mean in the physical sense." He tries again: "I mean, you are a good soul. But I think you're beautiful, too. In the way of looking at you. A very beautiful girl."

"That's a pretty aggressive thing to say," Tracy says, looking at him. She seems to be kidding.

"Crap." This comes out lightly, humorously, just as George intends.

"Anyway, if I'm beautiful I'm a beautiful *woman*, George."

"Oh double crap."

"Have you ever had a girlfriend?"

"No, just women friends."

"Any of them romantic?"

"Of course."

"Ever been married?"

"No, I hate women too much, loathe them. Ick."

"Ever had a gay lover?"

"Dozens."

Tracy burbles, says, "Come on. Truth or dare."

"If I say no—which is the truth—you're going to say I hate men."

"It's yourself you don't like."

"Let's talk about your problems for a change. Did you ever have a boyfriend? Or do you talk too much?"

"You are *so* aggressive."

"Sorry. No, really. Did you ever have a boyfriend?"

"Of course," she says.

"See how silly the question is?"

"I've gone out with three guys, long-term, and all three were assholes. Blunderbusses. Numchucks."

"I get it. You go out with blunderbusses, so now I have to hate women."

Silence. Then: "Geez. That was pretty right-on."

"Thank you."

"But you're still a pretty pissed-off guy under that laid-back surface thing."

"Bullshit."

"Aggressive response."

"Aggressive question."

"So how come you avoid your sister?"

George smiles wearily, face hot, gazes out the window at nothing, says, "Can we just listen to the radio?"

"Take all the time you wish. But at some point you'll have to just forget about her. Say, 'So be it.' Send her a Christmas card and don't feel guilty."

"Let's put the radio on."

Tracy turns the big cheap knobs and searches interminably for a song she likes on the crowded FM bands near Cleveland. Finally she settles on some woman singing about how she's not aware of too many things, and calls it an oldie, though George has never heard it at all. They listen to the music, but the tension in the truck is pretty high. George wishes he hadn't called her beautiful, though it's true, he thinks, looking quickly at her, she's started to seem the most beautiful person he's ever talked to or imagined, and this revelation makes him self-conscious in a way he hasn't been for years.

Tracy can't contain herself, one song is all they get. She turns the radio down, almost off. "Funny that she's a college prof and you're a truck driver. I mean, okay, I know you're more than that. And I know you're going to do a lot of cool things in life. It's like you're just waiting to clear the air with this family stuff. It's hard to grow past all that. I have this student in my Intro section who just started *college* at thirty-six. She had to work out this major fear that she couldn't *do* college. That she just wasn't smart enough, you know? And it turns out she'd been more or less told this her whole life by her parents—they didn't mean it, I bet—but they told her in a million ways that she wasn't as good as her stupid gorgeous Harvard sister and her football hero loser brother. I mean, I know these people. She's the excellent one. She had to dump the whole tribe. She dumped 'em. Said goodbye. Resurfaced a year later as her new self. Spectacular. She's the smartest person I've ever had in class. The best."

George drives a long time quietly. Finally he says, "That's a nice story."

And Tracy's quiet a long time, too, before she says, "And I think you're the sweetest guy I've talked to in about ten years."

❯ ❯ ❯

It's the right address, and George and Tracy are standing beside the truck, which takes up the whole curb in front of George's sister's house.

"Let's just forget it," George says.

"We'll tell her I'm your helper. Come on."

They walk up the neat flagstone walk, side-by-side to the door. The place seems so nice, so tidy, so Tracy Lynn, somehow, that George wants to just walk away. He's unpleasantly full from the diner dinner he and his new helper have just eaten. He's got clouds in his head, the fragments of several hundred planned and replanned opening speeches. It's absurd. She's only his sister.

Tracy rings the doorbell, and in one second the door flies open and there's an Asian woman standing there, looking slightly annoyed.

George seems to find himself, says, "I'm looking for Tracy Lynn Skinner-Peabody. Professor Skinner-Peabody. Or Kevin. Are they here?"

"Oh dear," the Asian woman says, her face opening at the familiar names. She's about fifty years old, George thinks. Just the kind of friend Tracy Lynn would have.

"I'm her brother," George says, to move things along.

"You look like her. But you must know she on sabbatical this year. She and Kevin in Argentina. You know this?"

"Ah, yes. Of course."

"We just have something for her," Tracy says, professional tone, delivery person. "We have a piece of furniture George would like to drop off."

George smiles, then starts to laugh, turns and walks into his laughter, trips back up the flagstones, leaving Tracy to chat with the woman. In a minute his helper is back, opening the rear truck door, and it's all the two of them can do to tip the $30,000 Turner breakfront off the tailgate and through their laughter onto the dolly. They roll it into the garage together, supervised by the Asian lady, who is really pretty nice about their silliness, who smiles and nods her head—the antics of brothers!—as they push the ungainly breakfront up against the absolutely spotless sheetrock wall at the back of the absolutely spotless garage.

The Asian lady wants to get George a piece of paper for a note, since he's refused tea, refused even to come inside, and though George has said, "Please don't bother," Tracy has said, "Thanks, some paper would be nice," and George finds himself alone in the garage with a piece of notepaper, scarcely believing he's about to steal the breakfront.

Tracy Lynn hello, it's George. This is a little
wedding present from us to both of you. Thanks for
being patient. Welcome back from Argentina.
Sometime soon I'll stop by to fix the gouge on the
side of this thing. Really, though, it's a delicious
piece. Come see us in New York.

The *us* just sounds right, maybe means Bergenstaedtler, maybe
Carl. In the truck Tracy and George giggle uncontrollably clear to
the highway and for several miles through more farmland. "I've stolen it," George says, suddenly depressed, "I've stolen a perfect Turner
breakfront and I'm screwed."

"Stolen it? You didn't steal anything. You refused a defective piece
and Carl the Blue Beret abandoned it in the hotel parking lot!"

They laugh, but not with quite the same silliness and abandon.
They roll through many miles in silence. It's getting late, and there's
the issue of the night, of where to stay. George is sleepy now, dri-ving.
It's near eleven o'clock and Tracy says she's not sure she can drive
the heavy clutch of the 12-wheeler, or any clutch, not really.

So she puts the radio on and sings softly to several unfamiliar
songs, sings nicely, looking at George, sings in that kind of serious
singing voice that young women have sometimes, good enough to
perform, if only they could do their singing a little more loudly or
in front of more than a couple of friends.

Somewhere near Syracuse, Tracy undoes her seat belt, slides over
on the long seat, and puts a hand on George's knee as he drives, puts
her hand on George's knee and sings as the big truck bounces mer-
rily, lullingly down the road.

"Let's stop a while," she says in his ear, and immediately, almost
like magic, there's a rest area, so George pulls in to comply.

Loneliness

Porter hadn't seen a whole movie in years. At his kitchen table he ate babaganoush and pita (both of his own careful creation), thinking rather hopelessly of all the prints he'd worked on of all the rushes from all the films he and his colleagues at MegaArt Color Labs had processed, then dressed in his good coat and big slush boots and stepped from his rooms to the gray elevator, yellow lobby light, and out into the blowing and freezing New York night. Forty minutes early for the movie he stood indecisively and bent to the wind in front of the box office, thinking how prices had gotten higher since he'd been, gotten much higher—five bucks was what he expected but the letterboard said *nine*.

At length he bought a ticket, put it carefully in one pocket then another, walked up Broadway to a dismal small bar at 100th Street (not a perfect neighborhood but his own and familiar and in the cold at dinnertime mostly abandoned). He drank a fancy bottle of beer quickly, asked another of the unfriendly bartender, drank that, listened to the TV, listened to the lone game machine played by the other customer, thought about rising prices and the stasis of his wages.

He got back to the movie house, still a few minutes early. In the lobby a line had formed. Porter stood behind a young woman with long brown hair as thick and glossy as in any shampoo ad, a nineteen-year-old's hair. He was at the end of the line, just against the doors, so when more people came in (laughing uproariously), he had to move up beside the girl. She eyed him neutrally. He tried to smile but something more like a grimace crossed his face. He thought she must smell the two beers, thought how his hair must be matted down by the woolen cap he'd removed, felt his mustache moist from his own breath in the extreme cold out there, wiped an arm across his mouth. The girl got disgusted in that instant and turned away from him, studied the poster beside her. Porter shrugged and thought, That's how I look to a nineteen-year-old: balding, old, dripping with snot, leering.

He turned so as not to bother her, heard her parka swish as she turned too, relieved of having to look at the poster. Porter could see her face reflected without much color in the glass of the coming attractions case across the narrow lobby. Oh, she was pretty. He was careful not to look at her again. He didn't want to scare her, remembered a night in Soho, back in Soho, back when he could afford to live there (when anyone could), another time when he was alone (just after Carolyn, and all that) but out stomping, drink-ing, dinner, a loud band someplace on Bleecker Street, coming home late and drunk, not stumbling (not Porter), marching rather, feeling well, not low with the solitude, but high and happy to be alone. Ahead of him on Wooster Street a woman walked slowly then briskly in her midi-length skirt, swish-swish in front of him, then faster as she noticed he was catching up. One block, then her pace quickened. Something in her fear made Porter nervous, so he hurried, too. He just wanted to get home. He wasn't thinking of her, didn't connect her fear with himself. She walked faster and faster, two blocks, then three. She turned to look, frightened, and broke into a run. Porter understood suddenly and slowed down to allay her terror, stopped. She raced away and ducked into a doorway mid-block. Porter took a few steps and realized she'd ducked into *his* doorway. He walked the block between them, opened the outer door—it was his building after all!—meaning to say, Don't worry! and to laugh, and to sigh their relief. But, elegant young woman, she screamed, which scared Porter so badly that he screamed back. She pushed past him and out the door, ran away down the street without hearing his explanation. He felt rotten with the incident for days, looked in the mirror to see how he had instilled such panic.

Terrible, he thought, standing there in line at the movies, terrible that she most probably still told people the story of her near rape on Wooster Street and dreamed horrified of Porter's benign own face.

The crowd from the first show came out quietly, looking serious, as if they had liked the movie. Porter watched all of them, enjoying their different reactions, moved up with the small line as the usher took tickets and ripped them. The young woman was in front of him, her thin legs poking from her pillowy orange parka. He made sure not to look at her at all. Not a bit.

The theater was tiny, only about twenty rows deep from the screen, and narrow. Porter took a seat second row from the back at the aisle. As he worked to shrug out of his huge black coat he realized he'd inadvertantly picked a spot behind the girl—not directly behind her, and a couple of rows back to be sure, but behind her nonetheless. Elvis Presley over the sound system. Porter got the coat off and arranged it beside him, studied it. Perhaps, he thought, the grand old thing made him look odd, somehow threatening.

The theater wasn't going to fill up. Scattered around the place were the fifteen or so people who had been in line. Four or five more couples trickled in. "Heartbreak Hotel" on the sound system.

The young woman took her parka off, then her sweater. Porter watched her, since she couldn't see. What harm? She wore a white shirt, lacy fabric. Her sweater had made a mess of her luxurious hair so she stroked it back, made a ponytail, dug in her bag for a clip, doubled the ponytail into a faulty bun and secured it. Her neck was delicate. Very pale. Her ears were sweet, too. Porter thought if she were not she but some new girlfriend, someone he loved dearly, he would kiss her ears and her neck. He imagined doing so. She turned suddenly and looked at him and caught him at it—staring, daydreaming. Damn it! He didn't want to scare her. He didn't want to bother her. He didn't want to meet her. He didn't plan to say a word to her. Had nothing the least amount bothersome in any way at all in mind. Instead of looking away he tried again to smile, but he'd been alone for several days of a long weekend and his smile was simply not in service. She scowled at him, looked away.

Porter did not watch her. He wished fervently for the movie. The young woman sat stiff in her seat. A pair of gay men came in and sat in front of Porter in the row beside her. They left two seats between her and themselves, one piled with her coat, her sweater, her black bag. They took their own coats off and piled them in the other. Porter studied the men a long time so as not to look at her. As "Love Me Tender" began to play, one of the men turned and regarded Porter, gave him a grin, kept staring happily till Porter broke the gaze. The man kissed his date, looked back at Porter. So, Porter thought, maybe I don't look so odd. He smiled at the man quite successfully, nodded a little to acknowledge him, a pleasant nod and smile he hoped would not be taken as flirtation, looked back at the girl.

Really, her neck was so delicate, quite small and strong. The stiff white collar of her shirt made her skin seem an angel's. She rummaged in her capacious purse and came up with an orange, which she expertly peeled. She put the rinds back into the purse and groomed the fruit, pulling strings of the inner peel one by one from around it. She broke the orange in two, pulled a section nicely from one half and ate it. Porter would have liked to have seen her lips as she ate, her wide mouth. He would have liked to be her date, let's admit it. Maybe her date twenty years ago. But he was an absolute gentleman and would not bother her or anyone else who asked as explicitly as she had not to be bothered. Yet he watched her.

She caught him again. This time he had the presence of mind to simply look away, no attempted smile, to just look away with the shape of her nose in his mind, a largish nose, bent a little, no real detriment to the marvelous lineaments of her face. She rose quickly and gathered her coat and her sweater and her purse and huffed past the gay boys and marched down the aisle toward the small screen, around the front row and to the other side of the theater, where she sat considerably closer to the screen than Porter imagined she wanted to.

He smelled orange in the air, sagged, sighed: terrible to have bothered her. But now the lights went down, and that would be the end of their lousy and unintentional meeting. Porter wished he could get the gay boy to tell her how handsome he was, and twenty old friends to tell her he was all right. Oh, they would say, he's quite interesting really, our friend Porter, a fine cutter of filmstock and a gentle man whom a lot of smart women have liked quite well.

He looked across the uncrowded seats as the theater got dark, saw the young woman rummage in her purse one more time, saw her rummage and pull out some half-frame eyeglasses that she poked onto her face as the previews began to roll.

The movie started as a love story but quickly fell into violence and madness. In it an obsessed man tailed a pretty girl through enough scenes that you were glad when in self-defense she killed him. Lots of ennervating music. Porter preferred less violent fare, had misconstrued the title, had imagined the poster showed a hug, not an attack (this ambiguity certainly the poster artist's intention). He looked across the theater in the dark of an alley scene, the stalker sneaking up on the heroine.

Now what would the young woman think, poor thing? Porter resolutely did not look at her and attempted to enjoy the movie. Not bad really; in fact, well acted, some nice nudes, interesting cinematography, elegant *mise-en-scène*, a good sense of light and air, amazing deep focus. The stuff about the heroine's family was probably the best the writers had to offer, clever flashbacks showing how she'd left the Midwest for L.A., for big dreams. But the music was just awful, screechy and melodramatic. And the editing was hopeless—timed by a philistine. When the credits rolled Porter was surprised to get the sense that people around him had liked the movie. He heard the gay man ahead of him say, "Wow!"

Porter had had to urinate for most of the second half of the movie because of the two quick beers up the street. The moment the film ended he jumped up, first out of the auditorium. He ran upstairs to the bathroom and pissed with some pleasure into a cracked urinal, hating the movie more. Done, and still alone, he looked in the mirror. He looked (he thought) tired but otherwise fine. He put on his coat and looked again. Still not so horrible. He pulled on his wool hat. Still all right. Something of a bumpkin, but not a threat.

He thought back over the movie's ending, trying to be fair. He almost never liked a movie when he saw it alone. Too bad his first in so long should please him so little. He thought of Janine at the lab, who was his age almost, robust and engaging. No reason he shouldn't ask her out. They were equals, after all, worked in different departments: no issue of harassment. A movie, is all. Dinner always so awkward. A beer and a movie, what was so hard about that?

Downstairs the credits-watchers were exiting. Still the eerie music. Porter stepped past a few smokers, stepped out onto Broadway, walked forty feet before he realized he'd stepped out directly behind the girl. His big winter boots were noisy. She looked back and gasped at sight of him, jumped over the snow bank and into the busy roadway, began to cross, thought better of it, leapt back to the sidewalk, fairly jogged in front of him for a block and stopped, obliged to wait for traffic. Porter slowed so as not to catch her up.

When the last taxi had passed she tore across the double lanes of Broadway, made the opposite sidewalk, looked over her shoulder, and headed back uptown. Porter watched her rapid progress up the block and saw her duck into Bailey's, an Irish place he'd once known well.

This isn't right! he thought. He walked back up on his side of Broadway, almost to the theater, to give her time to calm down. He would tell her. Apologize—quickly, articulately. Show her she had nothing whatever to fear. Then he'd turn and leave without bothering her further, without asking anything of her, without so much as buying her a drink. It just wasn't right to be so feared. It just wasn't good for this lovely young woman to go around so fearful.

After five minutes Porter stepped into Bailey's. Clank of beer mugs, lots of folks, a warm steamy closeness, buzz of the refrigerators. He stood near the door a minute looking for her, found her at the other end of the long bar, leaning awkwardly, too young to be served but waiting in any case for the bartender. Porter took off his hat and coat, draped the coat over his arm gentlemanly, held his hat, stood up straight. He found his image in the big mirror behind the bottles and fixed his hair. He looked fine: sweet, gentle, pleasant, nice, maybe a little lonesome. He made a smile, marched downbar to stand at the young woman's side.

"Hello," he said.

She looked at him, squinted, gave the strained smile of one trained to be polite.

"I'm sorry," he said. "I didn't mean to frighten you. It was all a coincidence, and meaningless. I'm sorry."

She smiled more, shook her head. "What?" she said

I m sorry to have frightened you."

"What are you talking about?"

"At the movie."

"Oh, were you at the movie?" Her face lit up suddenly. She squinted over Porter's shoulder. "Ricky!" she cried, and danced away to hug a handsome boy who had just come in the door.

Was Porter at the movie!

He had given his apology. He would respect the young woman's feigned nonchalance. She stood talking volubly to Ricky, a quick friendly hug as he shrugged out of his brightly colored ski jacket. Ricky did not seem yet to be her boyfriend. He was a big taciturn football boy with a natty crew cut and the number eleven on his chest. The girl liked him a lot, was lit and afire with her effort to please him.

Ricky wasn't half so interested in her, just listened aloofly with one eye on the crowd, the stud's lookout for other girls, for any girl, for a look at some legs in a skirt.

Porter stepped to the bar and ordered a pint of stout, which he drank rather too quickly. He ordered another, watching in the mirror. The reflection of the girl and handsome Ricky appeared just above the cash register. She was telling him an animated story, gesticulating, very serious, a hand to her forehead. She turned to look for Porter—the subject of her tale—turned to try and find him in the knot of drinkers at the bar. He crouched to be hidden by the patrons beside him, turned to watch TV. Basketball. Quickly, Porter was absorbed.

A time-out after a foul brought a commercial. The man next to him, a burly Knicks fan in a Con Ed uniform, shook his head at the team's poor showing, expressed his hope that what had occurred thus far in the proceedings was no indicator of outcome. Porter smiled easily and agreed—though he'd never liked the Knicks much or even basketball—then stepped back a little and turned to see what was next with Ricky and the young woman. Ricky was hidden by the crowd, but the girl was in the midst of pulling her sweater over her head. Her shirt rose with her arms. There was some trouble with the sweater and her hair. Her shirttails, white, pulled out of her tight pants, parted, and Porter saw her belly button, which was all belly buttons, and caught him unawares. He cocked his head in omphalic wonder and delight. Where had she gotten her tan? Her sweater popped free and she caught him again, caught him staring abstractedly at her middle. He turned back to the bar. Oh, stupidity! He was making things worse. He ought to get out more often—he was turning into a *pig*.

He should have gone home after the movie. He put his head in his hands, thought again of Janine. He must ask Janine out. He sat up, planning this, sipped his beer. In the mirror he saw Ricky offer the young woman a green bottle of beer which she declined, pointing unhappily at the door. Ricky waved off her protests and put the beer in her hand, began again to scan the room. Porter was relieved to see that Ricky saw no one to worry about, watched in the mirror as Ricky dismissed the young woman's fears with a little wave of his hand: enough of this complaining.

The young woman, liking Ricky very much and with no command over him (so Porter surmised), had to forget about leaving. She put her sweater down on the radiator over her purse and coat, went back to Ricky. He got her laughing, and her new happiness relieved Porter entirely.

He looked away, ordered another beer, decided to forget about the whole thing. Vile movie! Getting everyone worked up for nothing but the profits to be made at nine dollars a head. Vile loneliness! Turning him in to something he was not. He got to talking to the Con Ed guy—the Knicks fan—and they watched the game on the TV at their end of the bar. Con Ed didn't find Porter odd in the slightest, in fact happily told him his theory about the higher scores produced in these late-night West Coast games. So sweet to have a friend! Porter tried to forget the girl and forget women in general and forget Sarah and feminine navels and if necessary think of Janine, with whom he at least had some sort of chance at a friendship, perhaps a date.

The Knicks won in a rambunctious overtime brawl. Con Ed pounded Porter on the back, as pleased as a lottery winner, excited as a father with a winning kid. The beer had made Porter garrulous, too, and he was pleased to bark back at Con Ed, the two of them laughing, shouting with the other Knicks people, their eyes on the silent TV. Con Ed bought a shot of Irish whiskey and another beer for Porter. In his turn, Porter bought a shot of Irish whiskey and a beer for Con Ed. At length Porter looked back down the bar and into the mirror. Different faces, but oops! there she was, trying valiantly to get that fool Ricky interested in her, smiling, laughing with him and now with some of his friends, all in their football numbers. But how good to see her happy, after the trouble he had caused. She stepped laughing to the bar, caught him and his eye in the mirror.

Her face fell. Porter didn't flinch and didn't smile, but nodded at her happiness, and the two of them held a long reflected gaze that the bartender interrupted, taking her order. She ignored Porter then, accepted her green bottles, handing over her money (buying drinks for boys!), stepped back to Ricky and his growing group of pals. When she looked back, Porter (pleasantly potted, let's admit it) was still watching, interested in the scene in a kind of cinematic way.

Was he at the movie!

Porter sipped his beer, the best he had ever tasted. Con Ed was looking back at the TV, hoping for some highlights. Porter asked for a pen from the bartender and wrote quickly on a thick paper coaster: *Janine. Way to ask. A Friday lunch. Ask her Tuesday. To Campagnola's or quiet place by new theater?*

When he looked up after a struggle with pocketing the coaster, Ricky was at his side. Several of the other football boys stood around him, too, and the bartender's face was only inches away. "Time to go now," the bartender said.

"He's bothering my date," Ricky said, looking in Porter's eyes but addressing Con Ed, who looked on quizzically, not sure whose side to take.

"A misunderstanding," Porter said, knowing fully how close he might seem to being a stalker, understanding clearly everyone's concern, unable to find the words to defend himself, though surely he was innocent enough, surely, surely. "Loneliness," he said.

"He's been following Anne around," Ricky said. "Following her all night."

"Out, then," the bartender said in a thickening Irish accent.

Porter rose, shrugged into his coat, shook his head a little to let Con Ed know it was all a mistake, found himself hustled along the staring bar and past the young woman to the door and onto the sidewalk where the football boys pushed him roughly over the dirty snowbank and into the street between parked cars. Other types might have punched Porter or kicked him or shouted names, but these boys were chivalrous about their violence, stood unassertively and waited to see what he would do.

What Porter did was slowly stand. At his full height he brushed his coat and said, "I apologize. Gentlemen, I'm sorry."

The boys sneered for one another's benefit and turned back to the bar as Con Ed came out through them, bearing Porter's cap. Porter smiled meekly, greeted his compassionate colleague. He said, "Well, at least those boys have a story to tell their friends now."

Con Ed laughed and helped him over the snowbank, helped him brush his coat, laughed and said nothing, still not sure of Porter's innocence.

Porter said, "Those boys have a story for life." He put his cap on his head, shook Con Ed's hand, walked away down the sidewalk and safely home.

And he thought of the football boys' story all week at work, thought of the story they'd tell about him, told Janine all of it over Friday's lucky and leisurely lunch: the night the old team rushed a pervert to the pavement, the night Ricky finally fell for Anne.

Fog

Twice I have been lost in the fog in a boat, once with Cara, once with Peter Pearson and both times scared shitless. Cara's canoe the first time in Blanchard Cove (we call it Fast Cove) with harbor seals around us playing and snorting, swimming under us and coming up way ahead, dunking when we got close, coming up way ahead again, calling us out farther, farther yet, we paddling farther, they lurking, farther yet, two seals playing us out, though her dad had said, "Stay in the cove." Cara paddled in front in her bathing suit, a bottom piece cut high and a top piece too big for her, very strong colors in it. And, no matter what, I did like watching the straps of the top piece, the way one strap fell off her shoulder when she paddled this way, and the other fell off when we switched hands, so she had to switch the paddle and put her strap back up each time. And she already had a good tan that came up from Greenwich with her, Connecticut. We were new to each other, a regular boy from Maine and a rich summer girl, last July, not even a year ago, not even a year.

Now, this was at high tide and the tides in Fast Cove are big so it was easy skimming out and the sun was bright and we paddled all the way to the deep gut by the lighthouse, which is where we ought to have turned back. But there was time and the morning was warm now after the fog had moved offshore. We followed the two seals playing their game with us, but past the breakwater there were no more seals, just the sea and Great Island and Foster Island far away and whitecaps.

"Better go back in," Cara said, and we turned the canoe expertly and paddled but made no progress; we paddled hard but still moved out to sea, backwards: two powers to fight, the tide and now a big wind.

Cara said, "Faster."

We did paddle hard but the lighthouse zoomed away anyhow and shrank, and the shore sped away, and now a high sheet of clouds made the sun colder (but we were warm enough from paddling) and we flew out to sea, backward as hell in that heavy old canoe, paddling against everything.

"Michael . . ." She called me Michael. "Michael, we are getting nowhere fast." Not scared, not really. Saying more than just what her words said, saying something like, Together we are in this danger. She turned and laughed and we caught eyes strongly and of all the moments coming and all the moments gone in my life, this is the moment I remember most. After the laughing we just looked at each other a long time.

True that the wind was stronger yet and gooseflesh on my arms, and I could see gooseflesh on her legs and her color coming blue, and I thought she wasn't going to like me much after this, unless.

So I said, "Let's paddle over that way." And now the wind went down a lot and we made toward the beach at Mares. I thought I saw a seal but it was not a seal, it was a cormorant floating. The beach at Mares Cove was two miles away easy. By now we'd lost Fast Cove totally. Not a chance. But the sun was back. And it was hot on my skin and shone on hers and on the strings of the bathing suit she'd switched with her one-piece the second her father drove off, undressing and then dressing magically inside a towel while I didn't look.

"We can hitch back," Cara said. "Can we?" And then she laughed and turned around once again, and we laughed and laughed, laughed out loud, eyes locked and seeing the part that did not laugh. The straps of her suit both fell down and she crossed her arms to put them back and we laughed. She was sleek as a seal, she was, no great bosomy breasts on her, a good thing no matter what anybody says, her shoulders wide from swim team. Swim team and her ribbons she'd told me about when we met our first time at the band shell in town. And her hair was plain straight and almost red. Around her ankle a gold bracelet that I wanted to know who gave her.

"You be back by noon for lunch," her father had said. He would pick us up in their van. And help us lift the beautiful old wooden canoe—the perfect old wooden canoe, made by Old Town Abenaki Indians in the last century, her father had said, "So be careful as heck!" That canoe lives in their boathouse (which is as big as our whole house), gets used about once every summer if that, since they're all so busy with games on lawns and pool parties and what to wear.

And he would take me home. Then tennis lessons for Cara. Then a pool workout, one half hour, and clean her room in their cottage, which is big as the old Milbridge high school, twenty rooms. Then clamming, he said. Me in the summer, I just let the day come. Cara's dad had life scheduled so it was nothing but a day's work. And Cara whispered to him on her tiptoes, begging, and he reluctantly invited me for clamming at four and dinner at six. And he called dinner "sup-pah" to make fun of me, fucking summer fudgie.

Now past noon and Cara in big trouble anyway, and the sun back out, so we paddled slowly and just noodled and splashed around, heading for Mares on the tide. "Let's sing!" she said. And we sang a camp song of hers, I cannot forget the tune. *The sun came out and dried out the landy landy.* Is all the words I can get back in my head.

And just as it's going right, trouble again. The fog. Hot days like this it will sit on the cold water and move in, move out. First a wisp, then we were in it thick, then out, then very thick, and I couldn't see Cara at the bow of the canoe. And then out, the canoe all turned around and pointed that way too in just that short time, then in again, and Jesum Crow, in for long minutes until we were cold again, like ice. We paddled hard to warm up, and I knew which way to go for about five minutes, then I did not.

"Which way?" Cara said.

I shrugged when she looked back.

And she said, "Point to Mares."

I pointed.

Cara shook her head and pointed in the other direction. And that's what we had, just the canoe, and each other, and two ways to go, and one trillion droplets of fog. Smoothed waves carrying us, sea swells, not whitecaps. We paddled the way Cara pointed. We were blind.

But it was only just past noontime: so many hours till dark. Close to dark would have been bad. Still, even at high afternoon such a big canoe was small and the waves were sea waves, and they did carry us. Cara was a champion swimmer, I not a swimmer at all. I spat in the water and the white spot of it shot forward, so I knew we were still moving backward over the water, no matter how hard we paddled. If we were still in the Mares tide, we should turn around. If we were in the Fast Cove current, we were heading out to sea backwards again.

What you know of the truth, you shouldn't hide. I said, "We are going backwards."

"My father is going to *kill* me!" Cara was blue gooseflesh again, the mists between us thicker then thinner. I felt in a rush that I was in love with her, felt serious looking at her.

She had asked me out in the family canoe to see seals. She had begged her parents and done chores and basically bowed and scraped (as my mother calls it) just to get to hang out with me. Why was this? I didn't think her father could kill anybody with his little fake sea captain hat and their big house and making fun of Mainers. My father, he could kill someone. Yessuh! But certainly would not. What would he care, kids in a boat? My mother, she would be worried if she knew about the fog, that's all.

I said, "I'll take the blame with your father."

And Cara said, "Not our fault! It's this stupid fog! Do you think we're going farther out? We should have brought life vests!"

"We won't need them at all," I said.

"I love your skinny legs!" she said. Same tone of panic, really. So we laughed and stopped paddling, and she got both suit straps up once again and it was like she was angry then. She said, "What if we go out to sea?"

"Well, we won't," I said, but I knew the sea was who we should be worried would kill us, everybody knew that. The cold Gulf of Maine.

"I can't believe this is happening to *me*," she said.

"Well, us," I said.

She turned around again and we saw each other.

"It's only early afternoon," I said. "The fog comes in and goes out back and forth on a day like this. Or burns off all the way. So we just have to sit. Then we'll paddle like hell and be just fine. You have strong shoulders."

Cara leaned back toward the thwart and reached and I leaned forward far and reached and we just barely were able to touch fingers in the million drops of fog.

"I hate tennis lessons anyway," she said. But she meant something else. And sat up and faced forward and paddled a little, a strap fallen down again. I felt the touch of her cold fingers still. Her father would be angry, see her in that suit, late as hell, clamming would be off, suppah would be off. He wouldn't want me around.

I cannot say how long, but maybe an hour of drifting, not exactly afraid. Uncomfortable, my mother would say. (She drives the school bus in winter.) Damp and shriveled and chilly and nearly blind in the fog, except for seeing what water passed alongside our hull and of course except for seeing the canoe and seeing each other.

After a long time of quiet drifting, Cara turned all the way around, grasped the gunwales, tucked her knees and brought her feet around, turned to face me on the metal bow seat. Then she scooted down and sat in the bottom of the canoe, clowning, leaning back on her seat as if she were in a boat in Venice, drawing her one leg up, putting her one hand behind her head, and singing out another song.

What I did was paddle. I knew there were many hundreds of boats working the waters here and that the fog would lift at some point and we'd be okay, home before dark. Every lobster buoy we bumped or passed made me feel better: a person had put it there.

Cara demanded I sing a song. "Something stupid," she said.

"Bingo," I sang. "Was his name-oh."

And she sang "We are the Falcons! Brave and true!" from her camp. Her ankle bracelet said KIT. I sang the Milbridge School fight song. She sang "Michael rowed the boat ashore." I guess I should try to say how pretty she looked to me, but can't. We laughed and laughed at Michael rowing the boat ashore. No one calls me anything but Mike.

When we were just about out of songs Cara shouted, "Trees!" I turned (we were going backwards still) and she was right, trees, just when you thought the sea was going to go on forever. Pretty soon we were scrabbling onto some slippery, seaweedy rocks, crunching mussels, trying to pull the canoe up without scratching it too bad. After a lot of work we managed to pull it all the way to a patch of sand and red seaweed. We were saved.

Cara said, "My dad will kill me!" But we were laughing from relief and sat down (not too close) and for a minute the sand felt warm. But then it felt cold. And the fog was so thick you could bite it. Then we walked up into the trees where the air was a little warmer. I wished I had a jacket, even a life jacket, something to offer Cara. She shivered badly. And her bathing suit looked wet and shrunken and whenever she turned to shrug about how helpless we were I looked up the hill away from her.

So up through the woods until we came to a lawn, a huge lawn with no house to be seen. We left foot trails on the nice wet grass, walked into the fog. Blindly we found a little shack—some summer people's beach hut—a fancy little place for when they didn't want to be in their house, like the lean-to on the Appalachian Trail under Piazza Rock, only with glass sides and no one hanging around and no lock on the door and a little fireplace with a fire set to go and two lounge chairs with thick cushions. No towels or blankets or anything else, just a thing of extra-long wooden matches on the hearth. So Cara lit the fire and in a minute we were not cold. I thought someone would come if they saw the smoke, though these castle houses on these great castle lawns do stand empty.

"Kill us," she kept saying, like her father was crazy or something, which he was not.

I don't know, we sat on one of the lounge chairs each. After a minute Cara got up and played with the fire, then sat back down, but now right on my chair with her leg along mine like the side of a cold fish yet nice. And she said she was fifteen already. I didn't say but was fourteen. And then she said to give her a massage. I did. She lay down on the chair with her neck bent against the back of it and I rubbed her shoulders in front of the warm fire. She said she liked to get backrubs. Her friend Marcy was best at it because she did it hard but it didn't hurt, you know?

So I rubbed hard at her neck (but not too hard) and skipped her suit strap and rubbed her back a little. She said it was my turn. I lay down as she had and she sat right on top of me and squeezed all my back muscles hard so it hurt (but I didn't say anything). I felt her wet bathing suit and a drop or two from her fog-wet hair, but her skin was warm and I got embarrassed that I would get a hard-on. And I did get one. Suddenly she was done and it was time for me to turn around, but I made a joke, pretended I was paralyzed with pleasure and couldn't move and we laughed and I kept kidding like that till my misbehaving dick went down. Then we sat again side by side together and she asked if I had ever kissed anybody.

I said, "Yes, I kissed Weezie Warren when we were going steady last year."

"How far did you go?"

I put my hands out a little, like, This far, like measuring a small fish, one to throw back.

And Cara laughed and kissed me and we got our noses lined up and I waited for air and we pressed our lips together. Her tongue touched my teeth. We rested.

"I hate my father," she said.

And we talked about this man humorously while I waited to kiss her again. Then we did kiss again and lay back on the chair, but the thing was, I wore only cutoffs. I tried to turn so she wouldn't see, but she hugged me and there was nothing I could do. And she said, "You can if you want."

And she said that again. So I touched her chest, which was wet still from fog and swimming and all, and she stretched and made a fake yawn and her suit popped up and left her chest bare and she was all goosebumps, that's exactly what she was, and I just lay my hand over her chest and made a bridge between her nipples thumb to pinkie. Then she rolled around and lay on top of me and we joked and kidded. I couldn't even laugh right. That serious feeling was upon me. I couldn't breathe either, rolled her off me and we laughed.

As a joke I said, "You can, too," meaning to touch my chest if she wanted.

But she said she couldn't, then put her hand right on my pants. And it was like, like. Like what I don't know.

We kissed until my lips hurt like I'd been punched. And I tasted her mouth, a little like sweat and a little like candy, sweet. And she said, "You now."

I couldn't reach her nipple again, because she'd turned against my chest, so I touched her stomach and she said, "Go ahead."

Go ahead what? But I put my fingers under that tight stuff of her suit, the bottom part, and felt her hair there and she said, "Go ahead." More than the bathing suit and fog she was wet, hot wet like her mouth, like that, and splash wet and hot and I just carefully put my fingertips there. She said, "Go ahead," in a breath, so I felt very softly in that wet hot silky skin just a finger.

She said, "Wow," so I stopped, and she said, "Go ahead," and so I made circles with my three fingers and she said, "Okay" and "Okay" again, and I did this till my wrist was numb. She said, "Okay" and "Wow," then kicked my hand up and—I don't know—made a kind of sneeze with her hips—no, really—and said, "Wow" and "Okay" and "Now stop" and giggled like fast breathing and rolled so I had to take my hand out quick.

Oh, we lay there like that, and the fire went down, but no one moved. Then she did and we kissed more. And Cara put her hand on my stomach, which jumped, and then tried to put it in my cutoffs, too tight on her wrist and she just fought her way in there and kissed me at the same time and touched me right on the top of my cock and I was like *pop*. Everybody laughed at this, but eyes serious. Then she wanted to know how it felt and I wanted to know how she felt and we said tingling and bursting, the same for both of us, almost hurtful, and she said, "Love you." Which I tried to say, too, but it came out like just the vowel sounds in English class.

And the sun was back. We could see where the big lawn went— nowhere. Just a big lawn as big as a golf course. Her father would kill her so we went back down to the sea and got the canoe. Cara changed into her one-piece right on the rock there, no towel to hide in. I didn't look except for the briefest second and saw her thin bottom and long back and colt legs and hair wet on her strong shoulders, a fraction of a blink of a second, but a sight I will see forever and can see right now.

Paddling was easy this time with the tide slack and the fog gone and we headed off the island (Foster Island, as it turned out) and paddled like hell to the breakwater and gut where a seal picked us up and played us to the landing. Cara's dad was there, all right, in his captain's hat, with Mr. Witherspoon, and the two of them were almost done getting Mr. Witherspoon's Zodiac pontoon motorboat off its trailer. They were going to come look for us.

He said just what you'd expect. "Where the blue blazes have you been!" and "Do you know how long I've been . . ." and "Lucky Mr. Witherspoon was in the shop!" But you could see he was only relieved, kind of happy. "It's 2:30! I've been beside myself!" And so forth. And Mr. Witherspoon just looking blank as a cloud, putting the Zodiac back up on its trailer. Another day, another fudgie, his face said.

Cara stood up tall and crossed her arms and glared and her father didn't even notice that the top of her illegal bathing suit fell out of

her towel. She said: "For your information we were lost in the fog
and had to wait on the breakwater two hours!"

I thought, Jesum, what if the fog never came in that far? He'll
know.

But Cara just kept going: "You don't trust me," and "I can't believe
this after we just had a *crisis!*" and so forth on her part.

I just stood quietly by, very nervous. I thought we looked like kids
who'd just had a lot of sex, the most they'd ever had.

Mr. Witherspoon nodded to me the way he does and the two of
us put the canoe on top of Cara's family van while Cara and her dad
talked a very long time. Mr. Witherspoon (I know him, of course,
from hockey) did not say one word or raise one eyebrow at me—
nothing either way.

Then Cara and her dad hugged and the two of them came hiking
over, and her tennis was forgotten, and that I should leave was forgotten, that we were late, all of it, forgotten. And Cara's father even
gave us twenty dollars in town because we were *starving* (she said),
and we got to have lunch alone at the Sandwich Shanty. After that
we walked all the way back to her place on Cousin's Point, holding
hands. No one came close to killing her, or us, and Cara and I, we
had a whole three days and didn't get caught making out once, not
even the time middle of the night by her parents' pool. And right in
front of her father she'd hold her hands out like measuring the biggest fish possible: This far! And we'd laugh and laugh and her mother
would smile and her father would shake his head. What did he
know? A little farther would be all of it.

Cara and I, we both cried when she left and I cried after for an
hour, like I never have cried ever, standing in my back yard, even
with my father watching. Cara wrote me (signed *Kit* on thick paper
embossed with her full name). I wrote back (Mom bought me Hall-
marks). No phone calls allowed by Captain Fudgie. Cara and I, we

had a kind of plan if her family came up for Christmas. But then she stopped writing. And out of pride, I guess, I did the same. School gets busy and not that much to say in letter after letter when nothing comes back. Still. "Get over it," my father says.

With Peter Pearson, being lost was just a quick thing, not as thick fog, and we were on a pond anyway, but that's the same day I told him the story about Cara, and that's the same day Pete and I started being true friends, back about the middle of September, and now here it's almost summer again.

Anthropology

The Bar Double Zero was nothing Owen had dreamed. Dr. Clark was much more taciturn and plain unfriendly even than Owen's uncle had warned. And Dr. Clark was short, with a homemade haircut and wild eyebrows like hedges untrimmed. And dressed in polyester head to toe, pants and shirt from Woolworth's, no hat, knock-off boat shoes like some pretend yachtsman from home. Duct tape on his watchband.

And the ranch was like the man: scruffy and scrappy and seat-of-the-pants, tasteless and ugly and dusty and rundown, nothing but brown buildings made of chinked logs and old planks, everything wired together, the yard just more nothing, weeds and bent spruce trees and plumes of dust in a steady wind, all of this conglomeration of nothingness alone at the end of a dirt driveway four miles long and connected to the world by nothing but a phone line the same four miles long strung on homemade poles beside drooping electric wires. Not a girl in sight, not a woman. Just barbed wire and dust and planks and wind. From the ranch door emerged another man—the ranch foreman, Owen was sure—to stand beside the doctor and look serious with him, the two of them just staring at Owen. Not so much as a wave hello from either. Owen took his time emerging from his junker station wagon, got to his feet slowly, and ambled over to the men like a cowboy, so he thought.

First thing the doctor said was, "Can you ride horse?"

The ranch foreman spat.

Owen could ride a horse indeed, though not with great confidence. "I can ride horse," he said, suppressing the long lists of excuses and explanations and apologies that leapt to the front of his mind and imitating the expression on the doctor's face and his way of talking. Owen knew naturally to mirror whomever you met, not to give yourself away, but only give back about what you got, a trick of his character that had brought him a long way in high school and now college life, but that made it hard to be straight with people sometimes, hard to say when he didn't know something, hard to say no when he wanted to, or to say anything he wanted to say, really.

But for now he was only an eastern kid, no cowboy, twenty years old, just halfway through college. More than anything he wanted a shower and lunch. He'd ridden horses at Camp Monadnock in New Hampshire for two weeks at age twelve.

"Would you mind at all if we sent you out today?" said the scruffy doctor. "We need you to count cattle." And that was about it for their introduction, except what the doctor must know about him from Uncle Dick and except for what Owen knew of the doctor from Uncle Dick, which was this: the doctor needed a hand and would pay him ten dollars a day for a whole summer, ten dollars a day Owen wouldn't have much chance to spend if he was smart, said Uncle Dick.

Owen was smart. This he knew about himself and relied on. If he could "ride horse" halfway decently, he could figure out the rest. "I can go out today, sure," he said, or really his idea of a cowboy said, speaking with Owen's mouth and using Owen's body to slouch like someone who knew what was what.

The ranch foreman looked doubtful—that was about the extent of the drama. The doctor said, "Well, fine," and they all just stood there in the wind. In the air the doctor said, "I've been called out to Townsend for a day or two. I'm the doctor here around, as you know. Your timing is just right. If you can go out, Enzio can stay back and keep the home fires burning." Then, not another word, Dr. Clark limped into the house, limped back out with his satchel, in a hurry now, distracted. He stepped fast to his truck and got in and that was it: he drove off for Townsend, where he was the only doctor till Bozeman, Owen knew, the only one, and needed today: July 12, 1972.

Owen's heart sank as he watched the dusty pickup grow smaller for five full minutes and disappear into a great fold in the rolling land, miles away. Enzio said, "Come on," and the two of them, ranch manager and green ranchhand, headed back to the old barn. Enzio led out two horses of two very different sizes and shapes. The little sassy one, snorting and flipping her tail and pawing, was called Maria or Merrier—Owen couldn't hear it right coming out of Enzio's mustache. The tall, thick-bodied, soft-eyed horse with the scars on his hips was called Flake, which name Owen got clearly. Only Flake had looked at him warmly that day, and that, he thought, might only be wish fulfillment and anthropomorphism, two concepts from the school year that weren't going to help much here.

Without a word more, Enzio packed Maria or whatever it was the Italian had said her name was and saddled her with two modestly packed canvas bags showing much wear. "Bedroll," Enzio said patting the load. "You borrow mine. Food for your week, what I was going to eat. They get a handful oats each morning. Sure you water 'em. Love this Flake, boy. Do not gallop him, never. Topo is right here. Better show you a few things." And Enzio dug in the first saddlebag, found what he was after: two geographical-survey topographical maps, taped together to make one map, much folded and abused. He flattened the mess over Flake's willing flank, pointed to a pencilled *X* that was the ranch, said, "Pay 'tention," then, without letting his finger linger anywhere long enough for Owen to get his bearings, pointed out this spring and that draw, this canyon and that service pond, the federal fence line, logging roads, an old homesteader's cabin. "You'll find the ladies here and herded under here and maybe a few calved right here," pointing and naming quickly and speaking inwardly, no teacher he, no coach.

Enzio folded the map roughly and shoved it back in its place in the load. "Anything of yours you want you better get," he said.

Owen breathed for calm and tried to look calm swaggering to his car. There, he just pulled his backpack out, this bright blue and shiny bit of leisure gear. Clean clothes in the backpack, and a fat bag of pot, and three books he meant to read, and his map of Montana, and he couldn't think what else. Little camera. Pack of gum. Cigarettes—shit, only two packs. What did Enzio say about a *week*? Owen couldn't think of the questions he should be asking.

"Be prepared to sleep out under the stars," Uncle Dick had said. "And don't expect any luxuries." Packs of matches. He found seven on the seat and floor and in the glove compartment, shoved them in the pocket of the pack. His guitar would have to stay, though he certainly wouldn't mind having it—too embarrassing to march back to the horse barn with enough stuff for a Hawaiian vacation. Baseball cap, sweatshirt, work gloves, thank God ("Aw, Mom," he'd said when she handed them over, brand-new), pair of pliers from under the seat. He tucked everything he could fit into the blue pack fast and trotted back with the whole lumpy mess to Enzio and the horses. Enzio gave the pack a long, unreadable gaze, took it from Owen brusquely, tied it on Maria or Mah-real, about where a man might sit, between the saddlebags.

Enzio said, "Nothing else?"

"What's missing?" Owen said, raising the question from the painful very bottom of his existence. He thought he saw some ripple in Enzio's expression.

"What kind of saddle you like?"

"The most comfortable," Owen said, trying to make his fondest wish out to be a knowledgeable joke.

Another cryptic gaze and Enzio tramped into the barn, gesturing Owen to follow. In the dark tack room there were three saddles heaved over the wall of an empty stall. Owen pointed to the thickest and fanciest among them, but Enzio shook his head.

"No, really," Owen said.

"That is the Doc's," said Enzio.

That left two dusty and well-used saddles.

Owen breathed some more. "Which is best?"

"Neither one," said Enzio. He took up the closer, took up the blanket under it, nodded his head back at some leather-and-buckles tack left hanging on the boards there.

Owen took all that up and followed the ranch manager back out into the sun and together they blanketed and saddled and bridled Flake, who took it all stoically. Mare-Rhea twitched, but took her bridle, too, and a long tether.

"You will count cattle, right?"

"Right."

And Enzio walked away. Owen watched him, breathing purposefully, watched him stamp across the dry yard and into the house. Then there was nothing but a strong wind on a hot day. Flake gave him that warm look, and Owen patted the horse's big nose. And waited. Maybe he was just supposed to get going, which of course he could not do, as he had no idea what it meant to count cattle. He'd have to ask, should already have asked. Only a dope tried to seem like a pro when he knew nothing.

But then the house door slammed open and Enzio was stamping back, carrying a little rifle and a long fishing rod. Owen had never shot, and he'd never fly-fished. "These you better have." Enzio held up the fly rod. "Get sick of rice and bean." He held up the rifle. "See a coyote, phht." And tied them to Mare-Rhea's load, the rod broken down into two pieces like antennae sticking up from the saddlebags, the rifle just tied in like any old walking stick. He handed Owen two boxes, one of .22 cartridges, one of fishing flies that looked like so many brown bugs.

"There," said Enzio.

"I never counted cattle," Owen said, conquering himself. "What do I do?"

"One, two, three," said Enzio, no particular expression.

Owen felt himself being hazed, and grinned. "But beyond that?"

"You seek our brand in the places I showed you on the map and count, real careful. Take time if they are thick. Count brands, not heads, and come in when you got five hundred and ten. Count any dead, too. Maybe write down other brands you see. Flake, he know where to go. He been out there. Map is some help. Go in the places I showed you and find our girls and count, that's all. Any late calves, count them, too, and tell us where to go get 'em. Shouldn't be more than about ten, fifteen, something like this. You're on Forest Service land after the creek, so you'll see other stock than ours. Count brands, not heads. That's all. Takes maybe a week if they are close. Nine, ten days if they are far. Keep your landmarks. And just loop around and count. You don't find Bar Double Zero brands? Not enough of them? Trouble. You hurry back then. But don't ask Flake to go above a trot. He real slow. Plenty water this time of year. You catch fish? Burn the bones and all the waste. Not many bears seen here. But." And he shrugged.

Enzio helped Owen up onto Flake and pointed out a dry double-track trail that led into the soft foothills of the jagged mountains ahead. "The trout fish make good breakfast, you'll see," Enzio said. Then he smiled warmly. "I was fixin' to go myself."

Not so much as lunch in the farmhouse.

Flake strode into the hills up the trail, Mare-Rhea following nicely on her tether, and all Owen had to accomplish was to be comfortable on Flake's broad back. He held the reins loosely and rode, anger welling up in him uncontrollably. He hated his Uncle Dick for saying nothing about what an asshole Dr. Clark would be and what tasks they'd send him out on without the least preparation, and he was mad at Enzio for that cryptic smile, and mad at his mother for having the idea of coming here in the first place so he could "find himself," dumb stupid woman, and especially mad at Nancy, his girl, who was at this moment settling into her apartment in London, beginning her year abroad and the rest of her life without him, all broken up over him when he'd told her—how often?—not to get too involved. Pure irritation, all of them.

Owen rode into the hills, out of the dry grassland and into the tree zone, finally, and there he stopped Flake easily, just a touch of the reins and a soft word from his mouth. He climbed down, dropped his pants in a hurry, and shat a mess, such were his bowels from the road food and the strain of coming here, and now this riding into the mountains with no training, only Enzio's instructions and the doctor's doubtful gaze, shat a mess holding Flake's tether, worried the two horses would decide to turn and leave him here. He'd never be able to hold on to the tether, not ever, if Flake made the decision to turn and run.

But Flake didn't. So Owen increased the risk, but Flake stood patiently with his tether loose on the ground while Owen, pants down around his shins and workboots, searched the saddlebags for toilet paper, which he found (relieved—who knew what that creepy Enzio thought necessary?).

Up into the dry hills Flake followed the trail, a methodical walk just a little faster than Owen might have done on his own two feet, and slower up the hills, but never a rest, just a plodding, pleasant pace up into the afternoon, the wind blowing, the sky pure blue, the ponderosa pines reddish in the bark and tall and smelling in the air like oranges, almost, or something Owen couldn't quite name. His guts settled down and he began to think things were going to be as expected, just more on his own than expected. He thought of his cigarettes. If the trip were nine days that meant only three cigarettes a day. This would be a strain after his usual two packs daily, but a welcome strain; he had been meaning to slow down or even quit. Pot, too. He'd smoke less of that. Keep his wits about him. And he'd have no opportunity to drink any beer for nine days. All good, he thought, and swallowed resolutely.

He rode three hours at Flake's pace, ten miles at best, and came to a good-sized stream, what Enzio called a creek. There Owen decided the time had come for dinner, and after dinner the time to sit still. Plenty of light left was the best way to set up camp. He let the horses drink, then tied them with slack to a pair of aspens in what looked like good grass.

In the first saddlebag he found a big bag of rice, four huge potatoes, nine cans of beans, two cans of fruit cocktail, a bag of carrots, a bag of sugar, a can of coffee, four cans Spam (was how Enzio would say it), large bag of oats, like that, nothing wonderful. Plenty matches (a cowboy would say). Also a large pot and a small pot and a cast-iron frying pan, all well used. In the other saddlebag, a bedroll made of four wool blankets and a big piece of oiled canvas tarp, tied tight. He wished for his girl. He wished for Nancy so she could see how tough he was. Rough and tumble. But there was no one.

He spent an hour collecting wood, wanted to have a good high stack for the dark of night, now that he thought about it, nice dry pine branches, which were in good supply. He made a ring of stones tall on the wind side, built a teepee fire, lit it with one match, one touch, his pride from camping days with the Boy Scouts. Someone to see that accomplishment, someone along on this trip—that would be cool. Nancy always talked about his knowing how to do so much, gave him these compliments when others could hear. He watched the fire, built it up, let it burn down while he scooped water from the river with the bigger pot, worried about sparks getting in the wind: dry around here. The filled pot he put beside the fire on flat rocks.

Oh, for someone to see him. The cute freckled girl from that gas station in Idaho. He thought of her a long time while the water worked up to a boil. She'd liked him. Kind of young. He thought of his girl Nancy in London. They'd split up, really. He should make it official. Write her. Onward and upward, as Coach Riley said. Love 'em and leave 'em.

Owen untied the fly rod and built it and studied it and pulled the silk line through the guides and just wished it were a regular fishing rod so he could use it. He really should have asked Enzio if there were a regular fishing rod. He pictured Uncle Dick casting a fly rod (casting, casting), had watched when he was little, knew the basic gestures of the sport. He tied a convincing, feathery bug to the thin end of the line, brought the contraption to the river, dropped the bug in without any fancy casting, paid out line and let the water pull at it. There was fun in this, but nothing could be so hopeless. He tried a few flicks of the whole line, thought he could learn to do what his uncle did—smooth, long, falling, gentle casts, the fly landing like a living insect.

He flicked the line and let the fake insect drift. Of course nothing happened. It was just him standing there. Only him. He could smoke a little reefer about now, why not? From his pocket he produced half a joint and matches, fired up. He puffed just twice, nervous still in the vast and overwhelming new surroundings. Count cattle!

His ears burned and in a rush like a warm creek flowing over him came the pot. The actual creek moved by, millions of molecules in a crowd, passing him. The orange smell of the ponderosas, like a certain cereal from childhood? He thought to ask Nancy what she thought the smell reminded her of, but of course she wasn't there. She was in London. He'd said no to London and in that intense way of being with her this year, and he'd pretty much broken it off with her, and he'd done it for a stupid reason: he had the idea he would meet other girls and maybe find just the girl he felt he was looking for, a girl who looked like Florence Johannsen, his first high-school sweetheart, Florence who smelled good like these trees (was that it?), and whom he'd touched inside her pants memorably with his fingers just once. And who'd dumped him for Parker Wright, football hero. Love 'em and leave 'em. Coach Riley was an idiot.

The creek was so clear he could see every stone and every wink of mica. It flowed here through boulders and made pools and splashed and gurgled noisily, soothingly. And then there was Pelkie, Liz Pelkingham, with whom he'd kissed two hours unbroken once, they thinking they would beat the world record but not even close (Lizzie looked it up: two days and six hours). He was never in love with Pelkie, though, not like Florence. And then Mary Carter, who was Catholic and always talked about how that was *very difficult* for them, but Mary was very willing, as his mother would say, and they fucked in her family rec room pretty much daily for nine months till he had to go away for college. But she was full of guilt and had crying jags for a week each month during which she hated him and screamed at him, especially if he said anything about how it might be her hormones and not really him.

And then suddenly at college there was no one. Lots of phone calls to Mary till she got a boyfriend named McGrath. And if Owen admitted it, he had felt pretty bad, heartbroken even, and remorseful for his feeling that she just wasn't right for him, that there was a better girl out there. And now the same feeling about Nancy. He'd have to really think about that hard. What made him cast after girls who ignored him and reject girls who loved him?

His line hit a snag and he pulled gently to free it, then harder, worried he'd lose the fly at the end and maybe some of the line so that Enzio would think less of him. But abruptly it came free and he reeled in till it snagged again. Then a fish jumped downstream, startling him: he had a fish and not a snag. It fought his pulling, but came in easily enough. Only one foot long, it was, with red spots and dark spots, brownish and bronze on the top half, pale on the bottom half, alive and beyond gorgeous. He got hold of its tail and whacked it on a rock headfirst, remembering the motion but not the remorse from his youth, but the remorse passed and with a handful of rice and a can of beans the fish made a hell of a supper, flaky and pink, and sweet as the creek. He thanked the fish for feeding him as he had read that Indians thanked their meals, gave it that much respect.

For someone to see him now! Nancy. The marijuana was a bad idea, kind of a strong batch: after being high and happy for a while, now he quailed and quaked. He burned the fish head and bones and guts thoroughly till they were entirely gone and burned the frying pan clean because of the possibility of bears. And then there was nothing to do but go to sleep.

When he unrolled his bedding, he found a nice surprise, which probably Enzio had packed for himself and forgotten: a quart bottle of Ten-High whiskey. This Owen opened and sipped till he was no longer nervous and sang songs and stared at the fire and wished he'd never said those stupid things to Nancy. He did love her. Oh, God, he really did. He wondered what would be happening if she were right here, the two of them lying out on the bedroll—two bedrolls—watching the stars and she would climb on top of him the way she liked to do and so forth, till his masturbating was done and he fell asleep.

When he woke it wasn't yet morning. The constant Montana wind had died to nothing. He lay in a misery of worries under the stars, deep stars in vast space that assumed no familiar relationships (no Big Dipper, no Orion, no crosses or boxes or lions or snakes), only stars by billions receding from him at huge speeds (as he'd learned in Astronomy 210). The horses were as still as trees on their feet in the cold air, just their breathing to say they were alive, and something scrabbling in the brush behind the spot he'd cleared to lie on, and something hard sticking into his back. London was such a big city, with cars on the wrong side and queues for everything and funny apartments with heaters you had to pay coins into. Nancy had been so reserved talking to him—their one phone call—not cold but more like brave, having been hurt by him and having resolved to let him go. And he'd talked so briefly to her and wanted to get off the phone and pretended to himself he didn't care about her. Why? For this? This was the ridiculous adventure he'd planned for himself! Alone in the dark with a rock at his kidney! The cheerful fantasy of his hours driving here was all gone. Goodly doctor takes tough boy under his wing, boy amazes everyone with his toughness. And that out on the high plains he'd meet a cowgirl who'd beckon him to her warm hut and always love him and never be cross with him or judgmental and never expect too much and not talk constantly and not want to talk baby talk ever and want to have sex always, except when he didn't, and have an ass like Jane D'Arms's and boobs like Melanie Fulton's and longer legs (definitely her own beautiful shaved legs tanned dark

except starkly white where they met) and the face of, say, Julie
Christie in Dr. Zhivago, maybe mixed with Brigitte Bardot's face in a
postcard he once carried around for two weeks, and of course something of Florence J. And pubic hair tidy blonde. And the sensibility
and sanity of himself. And want to drink whiskey and smoke plenty
of pot and screw. His fantasy went.

Now he only wanted Nancy, and on her terms, terms that would
have included asking a lot more questions and preparing better for
life, like, say, this trip and this job and this cattle-counting adventure. He'd turn back in the morning, ride to the ranch house, de-
mand to be taught. He wouldn't be hazed like this! He'd go back in
the morning.

The stars receded faster. Some blinked. But there was the Big Dipper. He'd only been looking the wrong way. The combination of
whiskey and pot had dried him out pretty badly and he knew a list
of things he didn't have: aspirin, for starters. Anything at all you'd
vaguely think of as for breakfast. A pillow (and not this sweatshirt
rolled up). Band-Aids, if you got a cut.

A big crash in the forest behind him stopped everything, his heart,
his breath. But the horses were still, not a move from them. They slept
on their feet, these Montana horses. He wasn't as tough as all that.
He hated to be alone. He hadn't thought of it this way—unhappy and
crazy. He tried to get the happier vision back: a man on his own,
rugged and individual, unfettered by convention and conformity and
provincialism (great evils he'd learned about in his hardest elective
to date: The Modern Novel). If Madame Bovary were here he'd gentle
her sweetly.

He climbed out of his bedding and stood in the cold air and felt
himself brutally alone. He didn't even have a watch, but he felt the
stars hadn't moved at all. There was no faint pink in the east, which
he knew was the direction he'd come from. There was no leftover

pink in the west, as there had been when he'd lain himself down. He found the whiskey and drank some, pull by pull, standing there in his pants with no shoes and no socks and no shirt, and pretty soon felt brave again and clearer in his vision: a man alone on the great western plains. He laughed with this vision and laughed at the scared half of himself and at Madame Bovary, who let those fuckers make her feel bad about being what she wanted. *The snow was general over Ireland.* Was a line he liked from some other book.

He found his pot and rolled a fresh bone and held it a long while. Steve and Mark would be in awe of him right now. He'd tell the story to them later and leave out the middle-of-the-night stuff, except waking to drink whiskey whenever he felt like it. He sparked a match and Flake stepped away, surprised awake. And then Flake gave Owen that warm horse stare, pressing away from the light of the match, pressing against the flank of Mare-Rhea. Such a good horse Flake was, with so little to worry him, as content one place as the next.

Owen would tell the story to Nancy and she'd be very concerned and fond and fascinated, especially if he left out the whiskey. In the middle of the night I thought of you. He'd say. He puffed a little of the pot and shivered and put the joint out carefully and got back in his bedding. He was up an hour then, maybe two, smoking cigarettes, half of one of his precious packs, but fuck it, he'd go back to the ranch house in the morning. He thought over all the same thoughts and returned more and more frequently to a vague, anxious fear and his resolution to go back to the ranch house in the morning.

〉 〉 〉

The first cattle he came across lifted his spirits. Mid-afternoon and his hangover was forgotten. He'd drunk about two gallons of water and just baked the whiskey out of him riding Flake in the sun. How he'd managed to drink that much in the middle of the night was what he wanted to know. A new problem: the pulling of the hairs on the backs of his thighs as he rode in the worn saddle had advanced into a kind of bunching of the skin—he was getting blisters from the rubbing on his jeans, and supposedly five or seven or more days riding to go. He'd ripped up a T-shirt and made padding of it inside his jeans. The other worries were at the back of things, mostly how and when he was going to get to call Nancy and apologize to her and ask her forgiveness and love and fly to England, fuck the Bar Double Zero and Dr. Clark.

The ladies, as Enzio had called them, were in a long, dry canyon that opened out prettily into a flat field of stones and grasses and prickly pear cactus that fell into a charmed creek lined with cottonwood trees. Owen had let Flake pick the route at every place the cow path divided, and Flake had been right. Owen felt the big horse and he were becoming a team. He'd ridden on despite the night's resolution largely because of Flake, who had no interest in turning back, but wanted to count cows, would only walk north and west. Fifty-seven in this place, plus two late calves (Owen heard himself reporting the late calves when the time came, using just the language of Enzio). He counted three times, let Flake take him through the creek and up the hill to where four more ladies were standing, staring. All the brands were Double Bar Zero.

The horses drank at length while Owen fished the long stub of last night's last joint out of his bag of pot and put the bag back in his shirt pocket, just kind of let the joint hang off his lip while he consulted the topographical map. No problem there. Flake had walked them to the first corner Enzio had pointed to. The creek marked the boundary of federal land. The peak to the west was Goshen Mountain. He'd traveled some twenty miles. About ninety or a hundred to go, if he did Enzio's loop correctly. He gauged the distance by the map scale, knuckle by knuckle, twice. Maybe he was overestimating. Now, due west. He'd kept the view of Goshen Mountain as his landmark, realized now his loop would take him clear around that undistinguished reddish peak. So always he'd know where he was, and when once again he saw the blue-striped cliffs he'd know he was almost done.

He lit the joint and smoked it down, and after that the ride seemed like something astonishing, something out of a movie. He smoked cigarettes, failing to wait long between them, the first pack dwindling fast, the second all he'd have for five days if he rode fast. Okay, four cigs a day starting tomorrow. His legs felt all right where the blisters had started. He only wished he'd thought of saddle sores earlier and sat on his sweatshirt earlier or demanded that good saddle from Enzio. Piece of shit they made him ride on. If he rode seven miles this afternoon—a long way—if he rode that far he'd be at the cabin Enzio had pointed out, and maybe that would be a better night. Maybe a girl would be staying there with her flock of sheep or maybe there would be a girl in uniform, Forest Service, out checking on timber sales or something and lonely as Owen. And she'd be interested in the problem of religion and science because of a philosophy class she'd taken recently (Owen had written a paper on the very topic in the very class), and she'd be tall, so that when she sat down Indian-style in front of the little fireplace in the cabin her knees would rise almost above her head and she'd tell him in the firelight how much she loved this Forest Service job and they'd play poker and smoke her cigarettes (she had cartons and cartons) and drink whiskey and smoke pot and talk with their heads close together, and the little freckles on her nose would be like the freckles between her little ballerina breasts, which he'd kiss . . .

He'd only just cracked the whiskey when he correctly judged himself close to the love-cabin, and would have passed the cabin if he were in charge, but Flake pulled up to a dense growth of small trees and wouldn't move a step more. Looking around from up there in the saddle, Owen spotted the thing then. An old, old log cabin it was, with a door too low for someone even as tall as Nancy (who was short), the roof fallen in and little trees growing up out of the floorboards. The chimney was intact and the fireplace that had once been there was intact, too, right where the dream girl would have sat sweetly cursing and drinking before making love with him roughly.

Down the hill slithered a little brook. Owen watered the horses and fed them their oats and tethered them loosely. Gathering the firewood he felt the blisters on the backs of his thighs, high up under his butt. Not too bad. But as he built the fire the blisters felt worse. He dropped his pants and sat on a rock and contorted himself so as to get a look. And it looked bad—just raw skin for two inches on each leg, and pink all around that. And not a Band-Aid or tube of cream or roll of tape, not a thing to doctor himself with. Even to pull his pants back up hurt. Oh, he was being hazed!

He made rice and beans and Spam, since the creek was too small for any fish, he thought. He ate and believed truly that rice and beans and Spam were the best food he'd ever had. Rice and beans and Spam and cold creek water and the sun coming down and build up the fire. And whiskey. And half a pack more of cigarettes before he fell asleep, the backs of his thighs on fire.

By light of dawn the cigarettes were gone and the whiskey was gone and Owen cracked his eyes to pure remorse. In England he could have gone to Stonehenge and seen castles and drunk beer in pubs and maybe found Darwin's house. To Nancy he'd said, "We'll see," cool as ice, when she asked if he thought they were breaking up. "We'll see," he'd said, stupid fuck that he was.

And now far off in London, middle of the night, was some bloke balling Nancy in his flat in Kensington Gardens? Some stiff-upper-lip Brit? Balling her while Owen fretted in the night next to a cabin some tough customer had built by hand and furnished by hand and lived in through winters harder than anything Owen could ever imagine? An older fellow like that shithead she met once at the museum who'd asked her out and she'd almost gone? Like thirty years old and so polite, she said. An art historian, she said.

Owen's only profession was Junior in College. Beyond that it was all sores on his thighs and fresh out of cigs and no more whiskey and a whole mountain to go around.

Flake wouldn't go the way Owen picked, so Owen went the way Flake wanted, and they came on more cattle, just ten, no calves, with two from some other ranch. But Owen knew to count brands and not heads, and to write down the foreign brand. And carry on. He rode sidesaddle when the going was flat enough, and that relieved the sores on the backs of his thighs, but seemed to cause rubbing on one side of his butt, and hell if he was getting another sore. He sat on his sweatshirt and on one of his blankets, folded triple.

Back up out of the draw Flake walked, then along a high ridge for miles, Goshen Mountain implacable and unchanging and impossible to go around. A herd of antelope bounding away. A headache behind his eyes. The sky wide as the universe. No clouds. Sun on his shoulders, starting to burn. The wind in his face. He pulled his Yankees cap down over his forehead to stop the wind and pushed on. Nancy could easily be thinking of him right now. By the time he lay down tonight he'd have made thirty dollars.

Owen pictured a tuna hoagie from the University Deli in New Haven. A hoagie and a bucket of fries and a huge Coke, that's what he'd have. And play pinball. And go find Jack or Little Sam and get drunk all afternoon playing pool at Toad's. Or up to Hammonasset Beach and just lie there on towels in the sun. Nancy was 100 percent right. He was going nowhere.

He could have gone to London and now he knew why he hadn't, just as Nancy said: he was afraid of being with her. Afraid of what? It was nothing bad to be afraid of giving up your whole life for someone who might not be just the woman for you, but Nancy was the right woman and Nancy was correct: no one was going to be perfect. He was worse than some little teenybopper dreaming of a knight on horseback. He was a knight on horseback and when the perfect girl did come along she'd see a man with no ambition and no direction, just as Nancy said. And if the perfect girl ever got his pants off she'd find horrible saddle sores in addition. Owen had been drawn to Nancy at first just because of how she expected more from him and praised his brains (of his brains he was confident, still confident) and his ideas (when had they stopped talking about his ideas?). And her body was *great*—jeez, what did he want? It wasn't like he was James Bond.

When would there be some water for the horses? That would be the time to stop. He could write a letter to Nancy right now. Or faster, a telegram. Or send flowers, which you could do by telegram, he thought. Oh, he loved that girl and wanted to . . . no, get a grip, not really. And anyway, you couldn't ask by letter for someone to marry you. He'd have to fly over there and find her in math class and hand her a ring. With the thirty dollars he'd made so far. His folks weren't flying him anywhere, that he knew. Though Mom loved Nancy. Of course Mom did, because Nancy was just like her, with the same worries for his future. Well, he'd be an art historian, ha ha.

He tried to hurry Flake a little, kicking just lightly at the horse's sides, the two of them and Mare-Rhea coming down from the bare ridge into the tree line, many gnarled pines. But Flake flung his head back in obvious anger and just stopped.

> › ›

Next morning the sores on the backs of Owen's thighs were so bad he couldn't get on Flake. Their camp was by a high tarn anyway, with a floe of ice still lingering. The water was so cold he yelled when he surfaced after each dive, but he kept diving in because the cold water soothed his sores. He and Flake and Mare-Rhea had found thirty-seven more of the ladies, and Owen had counted them. No foreign brands.

After lunch he walked alongside Flake and they made terrible time. The horses seemed irritable with him walking like that, but Owen could not get back on without resting his thighs. And now his back hurt, too. And he'd smoked so much pot in the night (no cigarettes left, no more whiskey) that he'd convinced himself a bear was stalking the camp, that Flake was afraid in the night, too, that Mare-Rhea was about to bolt. He'd even spent an hour on a bad scenario: Nancy meeting an art historian with a smooth voice and big eyes and deep conversation. After that he'd thrown his bag of pot in the fire.

He'd send flowers and letters and telegrams and go to London and out-talk the art historian and then he'd find himself married—and not with the girl in the love-cabin, see, here was the thing: he knew he'd cycle back to his old rotten self. Really, he shouldn't send Nancy anything at all; he'd done her this huge favor of dumping her and all because he was jealous of her knowing so clearly what she wanted and not being afraid of being by herself in London. Among people. While he'd chosen Flake and Mare-Rhea and five hundred ten cows. Nancy was twice the person he was.

At the point the map showed as farthest from the ranch, end of the day's slow progress, about where Enzio had stubbed a finger, Flake showed Owen a huge gathering of cattle. Maybe hundreds. In the morning the counting would be hard because the brands were mixed—four brands, Owen could see just right off the bat. These he wrote down, drawing the shapes, trying to guess the ranch names. And calves in there and the whole lot of them pointed in one direction.

No whiskey, no pot, no cigarettes, sick from lack of nicotine, the hole in him filled with Spam and rice and beans and fruit cocktail, nothing to help him sleep but his thoughts. A lot of work to do on himself. He made a list in his mind. He'd stolen from the record store where he worked weekends. He'd wrecked his father's boat trailer and hadn't even told him yet. He didn't want to think about that.

Owen barely slept, afraid that the cows would trample him. He held Flake's tether at his solar plexis all night, and talked out loud to the horse. And slept in stretches of mere minutes, and woke, horrible dreams, a cow coughing not far enough away, or was that the cough of a man?

❯ ❭ ❯

Sores or not, Owen got in the saddle. Every roll across every bump in the trail and every rock the big horse stepped over felt like it stripped the skin from the back of his thighs and pulled every hair out of his ass, even though he was sitting up on two folded blankets now. He had counted two hundred nineteen Bar Double Zero brands in the big herd, walking slowly in among them on Flake's broad back, Flake really leading the way acre by acre. Flake had done this for years and years and years, Owen suddenly knew. He talked to the horse all day. "I'm not so tough," he said several times. And "I love Nancy." Flake did listen. Mare-Rhea followed along behind docilely, carrying all the food. They were a nice pair, these horses, and did their hard jobs well. Owen felt that Flake judged him a little for not riding the afternoon before. And he told Flake, "I wanted to give you a break." But in a hundred steps he corrected himself, got rid of the lie: "My legs were too sore. I'm not tough. I couldn't ride yesterday. I didn't even care if you got a break or not."

Anthropology. That's what he wanted to do. He couldn't wait to write Nancy and tell her. She'd agree: he'd done really well in two anthropology courses now, both of his *A*s to date. He loved to think about people and societies and history and tools and customs and specialized language. His best paper ever was an ethnography of a local rock band back in New Haven called Them Apples. He'd recorded their meals and their slang and their work habits and their crazy hours and their songs and their family lives and really liked the work. They had seemed so cool to him until he got to know them all and realized each cool guy had his troubles and his quirks and his ways that weren't cool at all, but fucked up and alone and tender. Anthropology. He could declare a major. His trip here could be a project. Enzio might be an anthropological study in himself. What was his story, culturally speaking? What made him come to America? How did a guy like that get to Montana anyway? Anthropology! He'd have a great job and live on an island like Margaret Mead, only he wouldn't marry into any tribe because he'd be true to Nancy.

"Anthropology," he said to Flake. Flake walked right to a spot mysteriously off the trail and there before them was a dead cow. The sight took Owen a few seconds to decipher. A heap that resolved itself into a cow, not long dead, brand of Bar Double Zero ranch, lying on her side, eyes pecked out. He stopped there a long time and just looked.

In the afternoon they found a hundred and eleven more cattle. And now they were two-thirds around Goshen Mountain, about. So. He would get back to the ranch with all the cattle counted in six days, and Enzio and Dr. Clark would be pretty impressed. He'd say nothing whatsoever about his sores.

After rice and beans and Spam he shot the rifle a while, the Spam can at fifty paces. He hit it ten times out of a lot of tries, so many tries that he stopped shooting, wanting to save the remaining bullets just in case. He wouldn't buy any cigarettes when he got back, even if there were a town to buy them in. He wouldn't even bum one from Enzio, even if Enzio smoked.

〉 〉 〉

In the morning in one group after the next along a creek (Bulletin Creek, the map said), they found all the rest of the cows, the full count of five hundred ten. Add fourteen calves. Subtract one dead. Call it a success. Owen wasn't tough, as it turned out, but he was capable of counting cows, which he'd come to learn wasn't about numbers so much as checking in.

There would be one more night, he figured. And he rode on Flake, Mare-Rhea following. The horses knew the job was done. Something different in their steps. He gave them oats and watered them at a stony pond as they got higher up the flank of the mountain and into pine forest, very beautiful with gray jays squawking through and chickadees and a brilliant blue kind of jay he didn't know but would look up. The pond was clear as pure glass, right to the bottom, a whole pine skeleton down there. Owen pictured Blackfeet Indians around this pond and thought about what it was they would eat and how they'd have to structure their society to make things work best and thought about how men and women have roles that are partly learned and partly determined by relative biology (he could hear Professor Erlach say in her kindly voice, maybe the only teacher who ever really, really understood him). Archeology was very cool, too, right up there with anthropology, and Erlach taught both.

Owen searched for arrowheads an hour, resting his thighs, and suddenly wasn't in a hurry anymore and poked around the pond and then remembered the fishing rod and clumsily cast it with no fly for a full hour just over dirt till he felt he was getting somewhere, then really thought about it hard and remembered the way

Uncle Dick would let a fly sit on the surface of the water and how a fish would take it. So he tied on the biggest fly in the little box, something that looked like a grasshopper, and flung it out over the pond in a perfect, lucky cast, the thin, thin end of the silk line playing all the way out for the first time and the grasshopper-fly hitting the water with a smack as if it were real and had just made a fatal hop into water, small ripples. And he let it sit, wondering if the Blackfeet had ever fished and how they did it wiihuuu hooks. He'd learn about them. Library in Helena, which must be full of books on Indians. And he could ride out here when his thighs were healed and find artifacts based on what he learned. And Nancy would be in London true to him and he here true to her and they would be reunited at the end of summer when he'd go to London and study anthropology on his own (too late for semester abroad, fool that he was) and go to Stonehenge, and easily get independent-study credits from Professor Erlach, who said he was one of the best writers and thinkers she'd ever encountered, said this in her cramped note on his *A+* paper about Them Apples, a paper he'd written high on speed. No more black beauties, though. He was done with all that.

Splash, and boom, and his line was taut and the rod bent and his heart beat in his chest and he had some enormous fish pulling at his arms. He remembered Uncle Dick playing fish and so played this fish, just let it get tired, it pulling against the rod, wily, trying to pull the line over to break it on rocks, then swimming at Owen, then leaping out of the water in spray.

Let me get this fish, he thought. To get this fish means it will all come true—Nancy, career, the whole life till we're ninety-nine, all comes true.

The fish grew tired slowly and Owen did get it to shore. He had to run up onto the rocks so the fish came out of the water. It was huge, a huge fish, spotted and glorious and pink and red and an-grily alive. Owen didn't want to kill this fish—a huge rainbow—and he quickly got the hook free and tossed the fish back. It hovered in shallow water a full minute, flicking its fins, resting, then swam off in a burst, healthy and alive.

Owen tried the grasshopper again, many bad casts, then a good one or two, but dinner that night was Spam and rice and beans by a big fire with the horses looking on.

⟩ ⟩ ⟩

In the morning Owen rode high up on three blankets of padding, the blue-striped cliffs in sight on Goshen Mountain, high, thin, cirrus clouds coming in from the west behind him meaning rain, he knew.

Back at the Bar Double Zero, Enzio was a different person. He greeted Owen with a great smile under his mustache, reached up to help him down from Flake, shook his hand. But Enzio was the same person, Owen understood. He understood that what he'd made of Enzio at first impression was wrong, that Enzio was steady, that he himself was the unsteady one. And then there was Dr. Clark, who slammed out of the house and limped over and shook Owen's hand, too, looking nothing but kindly. "Flake!" the doctor cried. "Muriel!" So that was her name! And then the doctor cried, "Owen Andrews!" A good joke, greeting the horses first.

The doctor and Enzio, they had known Owen wasn't tough from the start. And they were glad—really happy—to see him well and successful. And he said, "My ass is *roasted*."

And Dr. Clark and Enzio knew that Owen meant saddle sores by the way he said it, and the doctor bid Owen take his pants down, once in the house (a nice house, when you looked at it, neat and well kept, Indian artifacts everywhere, and old photographs, even a buffalo head; Dr. Clark would help him start his study of the Indians) and had a look. Said he'd seen worse. Said, "Get a shower and I'll dress those for you."

And then there was the letter. A light-blue aerogramme from England. Enzio handed it over, and Owen's heart pounded yet again. He brought the aerogramme into the bathroom with him and opened it impatiently and incorrectly so that the letter got ripped in half. And read it anyway, fast: Nancy loved him and missed him, but she had met an Irish boy from Dublin and felt that since as far as she could tell Owen had broken it off she was within reason in dating a nice Irish boy who was interested in biology and was premed at Oxford. Oh, Oxford, where else?

"Dating" meant fucking him, of course. Owen's heart welled. Eyes filled. He read, his heart pumping in his chest. A long letter. She told of other adventures, trips and museums and dinners out with a new gang and a sweet girl from Austria he would love who was her best friend already. At the end of the letter, again she said she loved him and missed him. "If I don't hear from you I'll assume you don't mind and I'll pursue this new relationship. He wants to get closer but I've said I need to talk to you first, or hear from you first. But if I don't hear from you by, let's say, July 1, I'll just assume it's okay." And she wrote she was crying now and had to stop writing.

July 1 was last week. Owen popped out of the bathroom unshowered. He found Dr. Clark in the kitchen putting dinner on.

Owen said, "May I use your phone and pay you later on?"

Dr. Clark looked at him a long time before nodding. Owen knew what to say to Nancy. He felt luck was with him. Facing a corner in the darkened dining room, he dialed the rotary numbers. Three in the morning in London, but Nancy wouldn't mind, he knew it; in fact, she would be thrilled. Owen had plenty to say, and he would listen, too.

But he was too late. The sleepy roommate, Bavarian accent, said: "Nancy? She's out with Timothy."

And Owen said, "He's Irish?"

"Oh, Irish? Yes. She's not been here since Tuesday week!"

There wasn't much more to say with the doctor there behind him and Enzio right in the kitchen. Owen dropped the heavy old handset into its cradle on the phone. This lesson was going to keep coming.

Big Bend

That night Mr. Hunter (the crew all called him Mr. Hunter) lay quietly awake two hours before the line of his thoughts finally made the twitching conversion to mirage and hallucination that heralded ease and melting sleep.

Primarily what had kept him up was a worry that he was being too much the imperious old businessman, the self he thought he'd conquered, even killed in retirement, the part of himself poor Betty had least admired (though this was the part that brought home the bacon). This area of worry he packaged and put in its box with a resolution to ask only questions for at least one day of work, no statements or commands or observations or commentary no matter what, to Stubby or anyone else, no matter what, questions only.

Secondarily, Stubby, who was now asleep and snorting in the next bunk of their rather nice but rustic staff accommodations here at Big Bend National Park. Stubby was not hard to compartmentalize, particularly: Mr. Hunter would simply stop laughing with or smiling at or even acknowledging Stubby's stupid jokes and jibes, would not rise to bait (politics primarily), would not pretend to believe Stubby's stories, especially those about his exploits with women. Scott was Stubby's actual name, his age fifty-three, an old hippie who'd never cut his ponytail or jettisoned the idea that corporations were ruining the world and who called the unlikely women of his tall tales "chicks" and "chiquitas." Strange bedfellows, Stubby and Mr. Hunter, having gotten the only two-bed room in the worker's dorm by dint of advanced age.

Thirdly, Martha Kolodny of Chicago, here in blazing, gorgeous, blooming, desolate Big Bend on an amateur ornithological quest. Stubby called her Mothra, which at first was funny, given Ms. Kolodny's size and thorough, squawking presence, but which was funny no longer, certainly, given the startling fact of Mr. Hunter's crush on her, which had arrived unannounced after his long conversation with her just this evening and in the middle of a huge laugh from the heart of Ms. Kolodny's heart, a huge and happy hilarious laugh from the heart of her very handsome heart. The Kolodny compartment in his businesslike brain he closed and latched with a simple instruction to himself: *Do not have crushes, Mr. Hunter.* He was too old for crushes (sneakers, he'd called them in high school, class of 1945). And Ms. Kolodny not the proper recipient of a crush in any case, possibly under forty and certainly over one hundred fifty pounds, Mr. Hunter's own lifelong adult weight, and married, completely married, a stack of two large rings on the proper finger, large gemstones blazing.

Fourthly, fifthly, sixthly, seventhly, eighthly, up to numbers uncountable, many concerns, placed by Mr. Hunter carefully one by one in their nighttime lockers: the house in Atlanta (Arnie would take care of the yard and the gardens, and Miss Feather would clean the many rooms as always in his absence); the neglect of his retirement portfolio (Fairchild Ltd. had always needed prodding, but had always gotten the job done, and in the last several years spectacularly); the coming Texas summer (he'd lived through hot summers in more humid climes); his knee (but his knee hadn't acted up at all—he was predicting, and predicting was always a mistake and a manufactured basis for worry and to be abolished except when proceeding from reasonable evidence, of which there was none in this case, his knee having been perfect for nearly thirty years since surgery after hyperextension in tennis).

Many concerns, more and less easily dismissed, and overshadowed all of them by Bitty (he always called her): Betty, his wife, his girl, his one and only love, his lover, his helpmate, his best friend, mother of their three (thoroughly adult) children, dead of stroke three years. They'd planned all they'd do when he retired, and when he did retire she died. So he was mourning not only her loss but the loss of his long-held vision of the future, the thought that one distant day she would bury him. No compartment big enough to compartmentalize Bitty, but a kind of soft peace like sleep when he thought of her now and no longer the sharp pains and gouged holes everywhere in him and the tears every night. Count your blessings, Mr. Hunter, he had thought wryly, and had melted a little at one broad edge of his consciousness, and had soon fallen asleep in the West Texas night.

⟩ ⟩ ⟩

The United States Forest Service hired old people—senior citizens—as part of their policy of nondiscrimination based on age and so forth, pleasant jobs at above minimum wage. And because they didn't accept volunteers for the real, honest work that Mr. Hunter had decided to escape into for a salutary year, he signed on for pay, though he certainly didn't need the money. And here in Texas Mr. Hunter found himself, rich as Croesus and older, shoveling sand up into the back of the smallest dump truck he'd ever seen, half shovels so as not to hurt his back, and no one minded how little he did: he was old in the eyes of his fellows on the work crew, a seventy-something, as Stubby razzed him, $6.13 an hour.

The crew was motley, all right: Mr. Hunter, assumed to be the widower he was, assumed to be needy, which of course he was not. In fact, the more he compared himself to his new colleagues the wealthier he knew himself to be: Dylan Briscoe, painfully polite, adrift after college, had wanted to go to Yellowstone to follow his ranger girlfriend, was assigned here last summer, lost girl, met new girl, spent winter in Texas with Juanita from Lajitas, a plain-spoken Mexican-American woman of no beauty, hovered near Mr. Hunter on every job, and gave him his crew name because constitutionally unable to associate the word Dennis with such an old geezer; Freddy, a brainy, obnoxious jock taking a semester off from the University of Alabama, fond of beer, leery of Mr. Hunter, disdainful of Stubby, horrible on the subject of women ("gash," he called them collectively), resentful of work, smelling of beer from the start of the day, yet despite all well-read and decently educated; Luis Marichal, the crew boss, about whom much was assumed by the others (jail, knife fights, mayhem) but of whom little was actually known, who was liked awfully well by all, despite his otherness, for saying "Quit complaining" in a scary voice to Freddy more than once and who for Mr. Hunter had a gentle smile always; finally, Stubby, short and fat and truly good humored. Nothing had needed to be assumed about Stubby, for Stubby told all: he'd recently beat a drug habit, was once a roadie for the Rolling Stones, had been married thrice, had a child from each marriage, had worked many tech jobs in the early days of computers, had fallen into drink after the last divorce or before it, then cocaine, then heroin, had ended up in the hospital four months in profound depression, had recovered, had "blown out the toxins," had found that work with his hands and back made him sane, and sane he was, he said. This work crew in Texas had made him so.

$6.13 an hour all of them, excepting Dylan, hired on some student-intern program with a lower payscale, too shy to ask for parity, and of course excepting Luis, who'd been crew here many years though he wasn't thirty, and was foreman—Luis made probably nine bucks an hour, with four young kids to support. And in a way excepting Mr. Hunter who in addition to his $6.13 an hour from the Seniors-in-the-Parks Program was watching his retirement lump sum grow into a mountain in *eight figures*. His $6.13 and a great deal more he was feeding purposefully back to Luis in deals on genuinely exquisite paintings by Luis's tubsome wife, improbably named Cleopatra, religious tablitas of the sort Bitty had loved so well, and so Dennis Hunter.

And Dennis shoveled sand with the rest of them, a wash of sand from the last big rain that had made nearly a dune in the shoulder of the road for a hundred yards, a dune dangerous to bicyclists and this a national park, so the crew shoveling into the small dump truck, Luis driving, if rolling the truck ahead a few feet at a time could be called driving. Dennis Hunter in comfortable and expensive relaxed-fit jeans, shoveling, which he preferred to the jobs the other Senior Program folks got: cashier at the postcard stand, official greeter, filing associate, inventory specialist, cushiony nonsense along those lines.

"Fucking say-and," Freddy said. "Endless fucking say-and. Why don't they drive down the backloader?"

"Then only one person would have a job," Stubby told him with elaborate superciliosity. "Five of us are cheaper than the machine to run. Even ten would be. Don't you wish your only job away, Homecoming King?"

"Fucking endless fucking desert of fucking say-and," Freddy said.

"Quit that bitching," Luis said.

"Spic," Freddy said, under his breath such that Mr. Hunter heard. No excuse, an educated boy like that.

"It is nice and cool today," said Dylan, peacemaker.

"What kind of work would you most prefer, Frederick?" said Mr. Hunter slyly.

"Love slaaaave to Sharon Stone," Freddy said unwryly.

"She's like, my age," Stubby said.

"She wouldn't like no Freddy," Luis said.

They shoveled a while and Dylan was right; it was a good day for it, cool under high cloud cover, a rare day of breezes in the desert. Around them here in April after a wet winter all was in bloom: prickly pear, cholla, century plants, scores of others, colors picked from the sunset and the sandstone cliffs and the backs of birds.

"Lovely here indeed," Mr. Hunter said.

"I'd fuck her so fie-est," Freddy said.

"I'm not so sure women like it fast," Stubby said slowly.

"From Freddy, fast is the only way woman gonna like it," Luis said. "The faster the better, and gone."

Freddy grew redder, but didn't say it. He'd said it once early on and Luis had scared him, just a look in his eyes that Freddy was not going to forget. Alabama football: tough. Texas border town: tougher.

Stubby put a cheek on the handle of his shovel, grew dreamy in a way familiar to all of them: "Sticky Fingers tour one time I swear I was crating the JBL's when this little spacey chick comes up under the tower and squeaks, like, Where's Mick? and she was so sincere and I go, Mick's already in the Concorde flying home, baby, and she goes, You *know* him? And I did know him a little, of course. I go,

He's a nice man, a little vain. And I look down and realize she's got her shirt off and she's got these goofy little boobs and she's dancing and taking her pants down. If Mick's not around, she's thinking I'm good enough!"

"Yeah, right," Freddy said.

"And she goes, The show got me so hot. And we go back behind the speakers and I swear her goofy little bush is trimmed off shape of a heart and she's sopping as the bog end of a beaver pond and I take her behind those crates and . . ."

"Penthouse Letter," Dylan said, risking all, and Mr. Hunter laughed for him, and Luis, though Mr. Hunter and probably Luis had no idea what the referent of the joke actually was. Dylan needed the laughs badly, soaked them up.

The Stones groupie turned out to be a long story, her twin sister and all, and everyone teased Stubby and threw shovelsful of sand up into the bed of the small dump truck, none of them working hard, but together making progress down the road, exposing its shoulder wetly.

"Oh Lord, I gotta dip this thang," Freddy said.

"You take off the gas cap," Luis said.

"Fuck a truck," Stubby said, and everyone laughed and laughed, as if this were the wittiest crack ever made.

Such an inefficient team! The likes of which would in the past have made Mr. Hunter smolder. But he shoveled as lightly as anybody and did not laugh at Stubby's stories and thought of Martha Kolodny for no reason he could make sense of, her laugh from the center of her heart and soul and her large frame that oughtn't to be alluring to him at all but was indeed. And her braininess—intelligence always was sexy to him. She was smart as Bitty and as quick, though Bitty would have called her noisy.

Luis said, "Dylan, what about you? Who is your perfect *mujer*?"

And Dylan blushed and said, "Juanita," with evident pride and huge love for her.

And everyone at once said, "Juanita from Lajitas," which was fun to say and which had become a chant and which they knew Dylan liked a lot to hear. Not even Freddy from Alabama would say anything that might harm Dylan-boy's spirit at all.

"You are like me," Luis said. "A steady heart and a solid love."

And Stubby, damn him, said, "Mr. Hunter, what about you?"

"Have you noticed that I'm only asking questions today?" said Mr. Hunter.

"But I saw you stalking Mothra. Mothra, Queen of the Birdwatchers Bus. She's a cute one, she is. Tall drink of water, she is. I'll bet she was one athlete in her day! Iron Woman! Anchor in the Freestyle Relay! Bench press 200 pounds, easy. What do you say, Mr. Hunter? You were gabbing with her nearly three hours yesterday in the parking lot there. You were! No, no, sir, you were! You're a better man than I! More power to ya! She won't give me the time of day, you she's laughing and shouting and joking! And she was scratching her nose the whole time, which Keith Richards once told me is the sure sign you're going to get a little wiggle in."

And all work (such as it was) ceased. Mr. Hunter made a game smile and smiled some more and enjoyed the breeze and the attention, really. He asked a question: "Do you know that right at the beginning of Plato's *Republic* there's a discussion of just this subject, of love and sex? And do you know that one of the fellows sitting around Socrates says something like, *I saw Sophocles*—the old poet, he calls him—*I saw the old poet down in town the other day, three score and ten, and I asked him: At your age, Sophocles, what of love?* And do you know what Sophocles told that man? Sophocles told that man: *I feel I have been released by a mad and furious beast!*"

The crew stood with eyebrows raised a long time, absorbing this tale from the mysterious void of time that was Mr. Hunter's life. After a long silence, Stubby said, "Oh, fuck you." Mr. Hunter knew what Stubby meant: the implied analogy was faulty. And Stubby was right. Martha Kolodny was certainly on Mr. Hunter's mind, Martha Kolodny of all women, and the mad and furious beast had hold of Mr. Hunter certainly. And though it wasn't like he'd had no erections in the past affectionless three years, the one he'd had this morning had caught his attention surely. And it wasn't all about erections, either, it was that laugh from the heart and the bright conversation and something more: Martha Kolodny could *see* Mr. Hunter, and he hadn't been seen clearly in three years nor had his particular brand of jokes been laughed at nor had his ideas been praised, nor had someone noticed his hair like that (still full it was, and shiny, and bone-in-the-desert white), nor looked at his hands so, nor gazed in his eyes.

⟩ ⟩ ⟩

At the Thursday Evening Ranger's Program a very bright young scientist lectured about Mexican fruit bats with passion, somewhat mollifying Dennis Hunter's disappointment. Oh, in the growing night the assembled travelers and Rangers and tourists and campers and workers (including Stubby) did see bats as promised. And among the assembled listeners there were a number of birders from Martha Kolodny's bus. But Martha was not among them.

Dennis Hunter lurked on a back bench in clean clothes—Hong Kong-tailored white shirt, khaki pants, Birkenstocks (ah, retirement), eight-needle silken socks—trying to remember how long Martha had said her birding group would be here. Till April 17, was the date he remembered, almost his second daughter's birthday, his second daughter who was, yes, about Martha's age. Five more days, only five. That bats don't get in your hair, that they have sonar, that they are rodents—all this was old news.

Then there was a sweeping presence and a suppressed laugh from deep inside the heart of someone's capacious heart and Martha stood just beside him. "May I sit?" she said. This was a whisper, but still louder in Dennis's ear than the Ranger's lecture. She sat on his bench and slid to his side like an old friend, got herself settled, deep and quiet, perfume expansile, put her chin in the air and raised her eyebrows, seemed to try to find her place in the stream of words as the passionate Ranger introduced a film.

The heavy narration covered the same ground the lecture had, with less fervor and erudition, but the pictures of bats were pleasing to watch, all sorts of camera tricks and lighting tricks and slow-motion tricks and freeze-frames and animation. Bats streaming out of Carlsbad Caverns, not eight hours from here. "Always wanted to see that," Martha said, leaning into Dennis. "Always, always."

"I thought for you it was birds," Dennis said.

Martha put a hand to her nose, scratched. "Whatever has wings," she said. Her other hand was on the bench close between them, and she leaned on it so her head was not a breath away from Dennis's. He smelled her shampoo, coconut and vanilla. Her henna-red hair, braided back into a thick lariat, her strong chin, the strong slope of her nose, her deep tan, her wrinkles from laughing from the heart of her, her wide shoulders, loose white shirt—all of it, all of her, was in his peripheral vision as he watched the film, which was more truly peripheral though he stared at it, her many scents in his nostrils, inside him.

Last night they'd taken care of the small talk: Martha Kolodny was an arts administrator, which title Dennis pretended not to understand, though he knew well enough what it meant: she was the kind of person he'd disdained in his years as marketing wizard at

Pfizer (years he then told her about). He'd felt the truth talking to Martha of something Bitty had said once: he had really grown up after sixty-five. Martha had patiently explained that she ran a grantswriting office that helped provide funding—not such huge figures as Martha seemed to think—for several arts organizations, the Chicago Lyric Opera among them. Dennis Hunter could surely appreciate the Lyric Opera if not so much the private foundations that made individual grants to artists smearing excrement on flags and Bibles.

Martha herself had once danced—modern dance—with high hopes. She was too *big*, she had said daintily, "My teachers always said I was too *big*." And she had laughed that laugh that came from the heart of her heart and smote Dennis.

Her husband was a medical scientist at Northwestern, both a Ph.D. and an M.D. His first name was Wences. He was first-generation Polish. He was working on neuroreceptors, about which Dennis knew a thing or two, from years with the drug company. The couple had no kids, for they'd married rather late, after (at her age) kids were impossible. Wences and she barely saw each other. For them, the passion had fled. "I'm caught," she had said. "I'm caught in an *economic arrangement*." Her eyes had been significant, Dennis thought.

The film ended abruptly. The Ranger-scientist took the podium in the dark that followed. A spotlight hit his face. Martha sat up, looked at Dennis fondly; that was the only word for how she looked at him, like an old friend. She whispered, "One Batman joke from this boy and we're out of here!"

And in a television voice the Ranger said, "That's the Bat Signal, Robin."

"That's it," Martha said, feigning great shock. She rose and took Dennis's hand and pulled him ungently to his feet and the two of them left the natural amphitheater and were soon striding along a rough path that led into the Chisos Mountains night.

"I knew you'd be at the talk!" Martha said.

"I'm not there now," Dennis said.

She said, "I can't get you out of my head!" She was breathless from the walk. They pulled up at the end of a looping path that looked out over the great basin of the Rio Grande under brilliant stars, under coruscating stars.

"I shoveled sand all day with the boys. Thinking of you."

"I love when you grin just like that," said Martha hotly.

But you are married, Dennis thought to say. He held the words back forcibly: what if she didn't mean anything romantic at all? What an awful gaffe that would be!

They looked out into the blackness of the valley and up into the depths of space and were quiet a long ten minutes. "Mexico over there," Dennis said.

"You know you can rent a canoe and paddle across the Rio Grande to Mexico for lunch? No customs inspection necessary."

He said, "Someone did say that. And at the hot springs, apparently, you can swim across pretty easily. But no lunch."

"Unless you brought your own," Martha said.

"And the hot springs are very nice, too, I hear. Nice to soak in, even in the heat, I hear." He'd heard all this from Freddy in the grossest terms, Freddy who said it was the place he'd bring a *bitch*, if there were anything but *stanking* javelinas around here.

"Do you hear that snorting?" Martha said, as if in league with his thoughts.

"Javelina," said Dennis. He couldn't help the grin. Javelina was the Spanish for what Americans called banded peccaries, Dennis knew, like little pigs, partially tame, sturdy little wild pigs that patrolled the parking lots and restaurant dumpsters around here for scraps. They were more cute than threatening, though there were stories of mayhem among tourists as scary as the bear stories in Glacier Park.

"There's worse in Chicago," said Martha, meaning just that she wasn't afraid.

"In Atlanta we have bombers and disgruntled office workers," said Dennis.

"Somehow I knew you'd be here," said Martha softly.

"I would like to kiss you," Dennis said. He'd forgotten entirely how this sort of thing was done, knowing just that now—this he'd read—now in the twenty-first century, one got permission for everything, each step, before proceeding.

"I told my husband I wouldn't mess around with anyone while I was in Texas," Martha said. Then, less lightly: "That's the shambles our marriage is in."

"Well, Martha, darling, a kiss is certainly not necessary to a good friendship," Dennis said, glad he'd asked and not just acted to a rebuff and embarrassment, though he was embarrassed enough.

But Martha kissed him, full on the lips, and he was glad for the Listerine he'd swilled and glad life hadn't ended and glad to remember all the electrical connections and brightened cells and glowing nerves he indeed was remembering from the bottom of his feet to the tip of his tongue as he kissed her and was kissed.

They talked and necked—no better expression for it—for an hour under the stars.

"Well," Dennis said, "I'm afraid, despite best intentions, you have kissed in Texas." He felt badly for Wences Kolodny.

"But I have not messed around," breathed Martha.

"On technicalities are the great cases won."

She said, "Do you want to take a little swim to Mexico tomorrow?"

"I'll unpack my swimming trunks."

"I said nothing to Wences about messing around in Mexico."

"That isn't funny to me," Dennis said.

But they kissed till near eleven, when the Chicago birders' bus loaded quickly and headed back to the birders' hotel on the outskirts of the enormous national park.

Dennis walked back to the workers' dorm with feelings he hadn't had in fifty years, pain both physical and metaphysical, elation sublime, ambivalence scratching and snarling like some enraged animal under his squeaky cot.

❭ ❭ ❭

Mr. Hunter no longer had the physical strength of his estimable colleagues on the work detail, but they had not his old man's stamina. With his steady work all day he outperformed the college boys, though Stubby could do more than the whole crew did all of most days in a single hour when he got inspired, which he did just before lunch this day, Friday. Stubby worked like a dog and demon and an ox, worked as if possessed: every cliché applied. He said, "We don't want Luis in trouble if this sand ain't up and off the road, boys!" They'd got about a quarter of it up the day previous, and already by noon this day two quarters more.

And this day, my God, it was hot. Plain, blazing sun. Mr. Hunter wore $400 chinos and a Gramicci T-shirt. His enormous Mexican straw hat (two hours pay at the tourist store in Terlingua) bobbed about his head to general hilarity, a foolish hat, but it kept him from falling over with heatstroke. The rest of the boys wore shorts and baseball caps, no shirts, and roasted in the sun, all of them except Dylan, who covered himself well against skin cancer years hence and advised the same for all, daily. Freddy the Homecoming King was going to be one spotted and speckled and scarred old geezer if he ever got past forty running his car dealership or his insurance agency: already he was burned crimson and sweating angrily. Stubby's Herculean flinging of sand into the little dump truck seemed to have caught the corner of Freddy's competitive instinct, and Freddy's competitive instinct trumped his more general laggardly nature every time. The kid *worked*, he actually *worked*. He said, "Fucking say-and!"

Luis shoveled too: that sand really did need to be up today, for Monday they started trail maintenance, and no excuses. Mr. Hunter got to sit in the truck and roll it forward down the slight hill in tiny and perfect increments, pumping the heavy clutch, worrying about his knee, then sitting there in the dry heat, no breeze, drinking from the great cooler of water, dispensing water to the other men when they came to his door.

At lunchtime the younger crew climbed on top of the damp load of sand for the ride back up into the mountain. Mr. Hunter slid over so Luis could drive. And the wind was pleasant, if hot, and the view was spectacular: otherworldly landscape, baked sand, a plane of cactus, bright cliffs of sandstone and limestone, old reefs in yellows and purples and blues and reds.

Mr. Hunter said, "Before I leave here, Luis, I would like to commission Cleopatra to do a large painting along the lines of the one you showed me in the Boquillas chapel. With that hunched angel hovering over Mary, do you know? And the little bald man."

"Santo Sebastiano," said Luis, crossing himself. "I will suggest it to her."

"I mean truly, the same size as the one you showed me in the chapel."

"That is large, Mr. Hunter. Where in your room could it go? And this would be a hard work for Cleopatra, weeks of time. For the chapel it was a gift, but you are not Jesus." He smiled like the only visitor to a hospital bedside: pity and sorrow and self-satisfaction.

"I am only a man, it's true. But I will pay five thousand for the painting, and extra to pack it and arrange for shipping to Atlanta."

"Did you rob a bank?" Luis loved to probe Mr. Hunter's wealth. He alone among the crew had noted the cut of the clothing, the whiter skin where an embarrassingly rich watch had lain, the quality of even the work shoes Mr. Hunter wore on detail, the gold covering all his back teeth, the tidy precision of his knee scars, this mystery of a rich man at common labor.

Mr. Hunter smiled with Luis: "Your wife's paintings are worth no less."

The crew dumped the small truck's twelve yards of sand at the head of the Gorge Trail, where next week they'd make use of it repairing a season of washouts and collapses and violated switchbacks. And one hundred yards up the trail, in the shade of a juniper tree, sitting each upon his own rock and looking out over the long gorge to a sliver of the Rio Grande and thence into Mexico, the crew ate lunch, each in his style: Stubby a huge sandwich of cheeses and sprouts and peppers and who knew what vegetarian excesses on thick bread he'd baked himself; Dylan a plain tortilla wrapped around beans; Luis a small feast packed in a series of paper bundles by Cleopatra, tortillas and three kinds of beans and slivers of meat and roasted peppers and whole tiny avocados and an orange and several whole tomatoes and tamales in cornhusks and more, always more; Freddy, poor bigoted kid, a single enormous bag of barbecue potato chips from the PX and his usual ungrateful snacking from Luis's bounty. Mr. Hunter didn't eat lunch, not anymore, but had a few samples of Cleopatra's cooking, marvelous.

As the crew settled down into what should normally have been something like a siesta, Stubby turned to Mr. Hunter. He said, "Where did you and the bird lady go last night when you left the lecture so early?"

"Why is it you ask?" Mr. Hunter said wryly, as the attention of the crew fell pleasingly upon him.

"I was only worried, is all," said Stubby, even more wryly.

After a long silence Luis grinned and said, "Tell us, Sophocles, old poet, what of love?"

"Love!" Stubby said. "You should have smelled our room in the night! What perfume! And perfume, my brothers, does not rub off without some rubbing!"

Still wryly—there was no other safe tack to take—Mr. Hunter said, "Do you imply that it is wrong for an old man to seek romance?"

"Not s'long as it's with an old lady," Freddy said.

"She's not as old as all that," said Stubby. "She's not yet my age, and I'm a youth, as you can see."

"Is she over forty?" Dylan said helpfully. He got embarrassed, bit into his burrito, looked out over the dry valley of the Rio Grande.

"Ah, forty!" Stubby said. "Forty is the youth of old age and the old age of youth!"

Freddy said equably, "How old are y'all, anyway, Mr. Hunter?" He leaned a long way, gave a short smile, reached and took another of Luis's tortillas.

"Three score and fourteen," Mr. Hunter said. "Seventy-four. The youth of death, I would say, if pressed."

"Y'all? No way. You don't fucking look it!" Freddy said.

And Dylan, too: "You don't even look sixty!"

And Stubby: "You do to me! You look sixty as hell, and that's a compliment!"

"What of love, Sophocles?" Luis said again.

Mr. Hunter could not help himself. He beamed. He said, "Do any of you really believe my private hours are any of your business?"

Stubby: "Do we not have the right to learn from those older than us and do you, Mr. Hunter, not have the duty to teach us?"

"Tay-ake her to Viagra Falls," Freddy said.

"Mr. Hunter has twice the cactus you have, hombre," said Luis.

"It's not all about sex," Dylan said.

"Thank you, Dylan," said Stubby. "And do tell us: What is it all about?"

"Blow jobs," Freddy said animatedly.

Dylan shrugged Freddy's coarseness off. He thought of Juanita (this you could see in his reverent face). He said slowly, "Closeness. Is what it's about."

But Mr. Hunter didn't mind that some part of this was indeed about sex, and that sex was certainly perhaps some of the closeness he was missing, and further, had the enlivening notion that sex and he might be in the same place this evening if he got off work early enough. But then there was the trouble, the trouble that had awakened him so early this morning and that would not be shut off in its compartment: "Gentlemen, let me state the problem: Martha is married. And my conscience tells me not to proceed, even as my heart says go."

"And what of thy pecker?" said Stubby, triply wry.

"My pecker says go," said Mr. Hunter, which made everyone laugh. He had never spoken like this to them and indeed not in his life.

"Then listen, brainiac," said Freddy: "Go for it!"

No laughter at this. Just an expectant turning to Mr. Hunter, who said nothing, sagging a little.

"Listen to your conscience," said Luis. "Listen well. If you spoke this way of Cleopatra, I would kill you just for speaking. For the doing I'd kill her, as well."

"Then y'all'd be single again, at least," Freddy said.

"Hey, I don't know," Stubby said. "This woman, this bird-watcher, Mothra, obviously she's looking for something her marriage isn't giving her. She's taking power here. She's taking care of her needs. She's unfulfilled. Who's to say she should honor this husband, who apparently does not honor her?"

Dylan said, "But she made a promise."

"What is the nature of the promise we make in marriage?" Mr. Hunter said. He tried to sound wry, playing Socrates, but this was too close to the heart of his worry, even under a tree in hot shade.

Dylan said, "That we should love, honor, and obey."

"The flesh is weak," Luis said opprobriously.

"The flesh has a job to do," Stubby said.

"I say, go for it," Freddy said.

A long silence in the windless day, punctuated erratically by the squawks of Mexican jays.

"I don't see how," said Mr. Hunter.

Freddy: "Well, the boy kisses the girl . . . "

And the crew, except for Luis, laughed. He said, "And what of your wife in heaven? What will happen when you see her there?"

"You're not really saying that," Stubby said, incredulous. "It's till death do you part. Man, come on."

"I agree with Stubby," Dylan said. "But still, the woman you're talking about is married!"

"Y'all should just go up to Juarez," Freddy said helpfully. "Soak that nut."

"It's not sex he's after," Dylan said bravely.

"Sure it is," Stubby said. He picked up a stone, weighed it, then flung it with an elegant arm into the chasm below them. "Get real. A man alone, a woman who likes him. I'm with Freddy: go for it."

"I notice that you say 'it,'" Dylan said. "But what of the woman, who is not an 'it'?"

"Go for *her*," Stubby said, conceding Dylan's point.

"I don't see how I really can," Mr. Hunter said.

"There are many women in the world," Luis said. "You do not need to break God's law."

The others, except Mr. Hunter, hadn't seen Luis as religious till now. The air grew more serious. Everyone stared off, each in his own thoughts.

Until this from Stubby: "Actually, there's probably more here than the moral question. You've really fallen for this chick, you know? How are you going to feel if it goes further and then—boom—she's off to Chicago and back to her husband? Leaves you alone! That's going to be a blow, Dennis!"

"When Tina broke up with me . . ." Freddy said. The others waited, but that was all he managed. Freddy looked off into the sky, and for the first time you could see his heart in his face and think of him as tender.

"There might be that kind of price," Stubby said.

"This is good advice," said Mr. Hunter. "I don't know if I could stand the aftermath of any one-night stand."

Stubby slid off his rock, leaned back against it, closed his eyes. Dylan lay down, chewing a twig. Luis stood, stretched, patted Mr. Hunter's shoulder, walked up the path to be alone. Luis prayed after lunch, Mr. Hunter knew. Freddy you might think was softly weeping if you didn't know what a tough customer he was.

Mr. Hunter had made up his mind: no married woman for him.

〉 〉 〉

Martha an athlete, Stubby had joked, and so she was: forty-seven years old, Dennis Hunter's height and weight, and walked with the physical confidence of an athlete, looked in her shorts and stretch top as if she might jump up and fly at any moment. But in Dennis's little rental car her folded legs seemed delicate and soft. Her skin was beautiful to him, and her smell, and her voice. "I couldn't sleep all last night," she said.

"I could barely work today," he said.

The other talk on the hour's drive to Hot Springs Canyon was about the landscape of the park, and they didn't need to say much for looking at that landscape, the great buttes and cliffs and mesas miles away and unmoving. Martha read from her guidebook: "The park is 708,221 acres."

Dennis Hunter hadn't known that.

She read: "The Rio Grande was known to the Spanish conquistadors as the Great River of the North, and to the early pioneers as the River of Ghosts."

"I'm told this was Comanche territory," Dennis said. Luis had said so.

Martha nodded her head, then shook it, then nodded it. "Comanche country," she repeated, saying it from the heart of her heart, where her laughter came from.

Oh God, and Dennis felt his heart flowing out to her entirely, yet not leaving his rib cage at all. They drove slowly through the great basin of the River of Ghosts, past the Chisos Mountains. A pickup truck zoomed up from behind, passed easily, zoomed out of sight, New Mexico plates. Dennis thought about how easily he could declare his love and ask dear Martha her intentions. Perhaps Wences was out. Perhaps a split was imminent. How ask? Dennis said, "Chisos means something like ghostly in the Apache language." Luis had told him that, too.

Just quietly driving along, looking at the landscape. "Yes, it is," Martha said. "Ghostly, all right." She put her hands up in a gesture of amazement. She'd taken off her rings. "Living things don't belong here. Not people certainly."

Dennis felt himself and the car almost lifting off the pavement. Not that he was faint, not at all; he felt more present if anything, floating car and all, with warm blood in his air-conditioned face and something humming in him, thighs to lungs. She'd taken off her rings. Dennis had never taken his ring off, not once for any reason, not since the night it went on his finger, June 11, 1947.

He said, "I've seen javelina, mule deer, pronghorn antelope, and a gray fox since I've been here. Also, Luis showed me the droppings of a bobcat and a raccoon and owls."

And just then a roadrunner zipped diagonally across the road in front of them, stiff posture a little comical, even somehow portentous, even to pragmatic Dennis.

Martha Kolodny shifted a little toward him, really interested in what he'd seen and what he knew. She said, "I've seen a lot, too: roadrunner, elf owl, Harris's hawk (I saw a pair), Inca dove, ladderback and golden-fronted woodpeckers, verdin, a hooded oriole maybe, pyrrhuloxia, vermilion flycatcher, a varied bunting (I think, I hope, my prize of the trip), an ash-throated flycatcher, canyon wrens (I heard them only), other wrens, a curved-billed thrasher, sage thrashers, many sparrows, a great-tailed grackle."

"You've got the list by heart," Dennis said, afloat in adoration.

She smiled, plainly pleased with his fascination and infatuation. She said, "All new additions to my life list and not one of which is found in Chicago, or much of anywhere but here."

In the small canyon where the hot springs lay they walked in the hot sun along sea-bed cliffs, striated layers of the ages thrown up by earth forces at odd angles. Martha heard immediately a great horned owl, and got it calling to her by hooting saucily. Dennis Hunter floated, he floated along the dry path and felt that Martha floated, too.

Together they inspected the abandoned ruins of the old hotel and store there, the hotel and store Martha had read aloud about from her booklet. Together they found the petroglyphs she'd read about, and walked along the path, a Comanche path that had become a commercial enterprise's trail to the hot springs, now but a park path for tourists. Martha took Dennis's hand. He wanted to declare his love. How old-fashioned he knew he was! She'd laugh at him, he thought, and this laugh would come from her teeth and not her heart.

The path descended between thick reeds and willows and the canyon wall. Soon Martha stopped, put a finger in the air. "Hear the river?"

Yes, Dennis heard it, a rushing sound ahead. Martha's hand in his, dry hands casually clasped, pressure of fingers in a small rhythm, a pulse of recognition: something profound between them.

A group of four British-sounding tourists with wet hair and mussed clothing came up the path. Their presence explained the one other car back at the end of the dusty and eroded canyon road. Dennis let go Martha's hand, oh, casually.

Approaching, a tall man with wire glasses said, "There's an owl up in the cliff." He pointed high in the sandstone bluff. "Just there."

Martha saw the big bird immediately, and pointed to it for Dennis's sake. When he saw it he was amazed at its size. He'd been seeking something smaller.

"Bloke's calling a mate," said the tall Britisher. His friends nodded.

A pretty young woman said, "We've heard her response."

And the owl, on cue, hooted spookily. Across the river came another bird's hoot.

Martha took Dennis's hand and pulled him along. "River of British Ghosts," she said.

Dennis couldn't get the words as the Rio Grande came into view: "Doesn't it . . . isn't it . . . doesn't this just . . . *tickle* you?" That was pathetic. He thought and tried again: "This little sprite of a muddy river, this ancient flow, this reed-bound oasis? That this is the famous border?"

"Dennis, I don't know what to do."

"That that is Mexico over there?"

"May I see you in Atlanta?"

They stopped there on the plain and dusty rock—flat, polished sandstone, solidified mud really—they stopped and held hands and looked at the river and could not look at each other.

She said, "What is this between us?"

Dennis could think of a word for what was between them. It was passion, nothing less, on the one hand, and her husband, nothing less, on the other, both between them and no way to say a word at this moment about either. He let a long squeeze of her hand say what it could, then pulled her along. Brightly, he said, "I expected gun turrets and chainlink fence and border stations."

"Well, there's nothing but desert for hundreds of miles. They just don't watch much here."

Pleasingly, no other soul occupied the hot springs, a steady gush of very hot water rising up out of a deteriorated square culvert built a century past. The buildings were gone, swept away by floods, they must have been. But one foundation remained, and formed a sort of large bathtub, well, enormous, maybe the size of a patio. In the hot air of the day the water didn't steam at all. A kind of soft moss grew in there.

Martha sat on a rock and took her shoes off. Dennis liked her feet. He wondered if Wences liked her feet. He liked her knees very much. He liked that she was so strong and big, he did very much, so unlike Bitty, who was a bone. He liked the fatty dimpling of

Martha's thighs in her black shorts. She dipped her feet in. "Wow, hot," she said.

"Maybe too hot for today?" Dennis said.

"No, no, it's wonderful! And then the river will feel cold," she said. "A blessing," she said. Then: "Well, no one's around." And she pulled off her shirt, just like that, and clicked something between her breasts to make her bra come loose, and shed it, then stepped out of her shorts and then her lacy panties (worn for him, he was startled to realize) and slipped into the hot water in a fluid motion, Dennis more or less looking away, looking more or less upward at the cliff (cliff swallows up there).

"I'm not sitting here alone," Martha said.

So Dennis tried a fluid kind of stripping like hers, but ended up hopping on one foot, trying to get his pants past his ankles, but stripped and hopped, and slid into the hot water, self-conscious about his old body, the way his skin had got loose, the spots of him.

"It's love between us," he said, which was not the same as declaring love. "And that you are married," he said.

"No touching in Texas," said Martha, far too lightly.

The water was shallow and she sat up to her waist and bare-breasted in the hot water and not exactly young herself. The hot water was gentle and very hot and melted them both, turned them red like lobsters.

"Swim," said Martha. And she climbed out of the pool down old steps into the river and dropped herself into the current. Stroke stroke out of the current and she was standing on the bottom again, waist deep. She was forty-seven and married and standing waist deep and naked in the Rio Grande River not twenty feet from Mexico. Dennis felt her gaze, thought of his knee, considered Wences, heard Luis's stern voice, heard Freddy's (*Go for it*), heard Bitty's funny laugh, thought of his three children, heard his daughter Candy

(*Daddy, I know mother would* want *you to date*) and followed Martha, climbed in the river after her, enjoying the cold of it after the scalding spring. Stroke, stroke, stroke, he was being swept away in the current, pictured himself washed up on a flat rock dead and naked miles downstream. But Martha got hold of his hand laughing and they stood waist deep together in the stream rushing past, silty, sweetly warm water.

"I'll get our stuff," Martha said.

She swam back and bundled everything—large towels, clothes, binoculars, bottle of wine—and easily swam with one arm in the air till she was back by Dennis Hunter's side, holding the bundle all in front of her chest, dry, and if not absolutely dry, what difference? It would dry in seconds in the sun and parched air.

Suddenly she said, "The American Association of Arts Administrators conference is in Atlanta this June." They stood in the flow of the river. "I could stay a week with you," she said. "Maybe more. It's June. Two months from now, only."

"After that?" Dennis said.

Solemnly: "We shall see what we shall see." Then she laughed from the heart of the heart of her and Dennis laughed and stumbled and they made their way through the water to Mexico.

"I hope no one shoots us going back," Dennis said.

They made the rocky shore in Mexico and walked, not far, walked in Mexico until they were out of sight of the hot springs across the river, and right there under the late sun she spread the blanket and right there hugged him naked and the two older Americans in Mexico kissed and Dennis Hunter was a young man again—no, really—a boy in love, a tanned and buff shoveler of sand, a repairer of trails, a knower of animals, a listener to birds, anything but a widower alone in Atlanta the rest of his miserable days, miserable days alone.

ACKNOWLEDGMENTS

Special thanks to the University of Maine at Farmington and to the Ohio State University for crucial release time. Warm thanks to the MacDowell Colony for time to think and write. Fondest thanks to my friends and colleagues and teachers and editors and agents and especially to my parents and siblings and in-laws and nieces and nephews—none of them anything like the people imagined in this book.

Grateful acknowledgment to the editors of the publications in which these stories first appeared: *Fourteen Hills*: "Thanksgiving"; *Whetstone*: "Blues Machine"; *Harper's*: "A Job at Little Henry's"; *Witness*: "Taughannock Falls"; *Missouri Review*: "Fredonia"; *Whetstone*: "Loneliness"; *Another Chicago Magazine*: "Fog"; *American Literary Review*: "Anthropology"; *Atlantic Monthly*: "Big Bend."

The Flannery O'Connor Award for Short Fiction

David Walton, *Evening Out*
Leigh Allison Wilson, *From the Bottom Up*
Sandra Thompson, *Close-Ups*
Susan Neville, *The Invention of Flight*
Mary Hood, *How Far She Went*
François Camoin, *Why Men Are Afraid of Women*
Molly Giles, *Rough Translations*
Daniel Curley, *Living with Snakes*
Peter Meinke, *The Piano Tuner*
Tony Ardizzone, *The Evening News*
Salvatore La Puma, *The Boys of Bensonhurst*
Melissa Pritchard, *Spirit Seizures*
Philip F. Deaver, *Silent Retreats*
Gail Galloway Adams, *The Purchase of Order*
Carole L. Glickfeld, *Useful Gifts*
Antonya Nelson, *The Expendables*
Nancy Zafris, *The People I Know*
Debra Monroe, *The Source of Trouble*
Robert H. Abel, *Ghost Traps*
T. M. McNally, *Low Flying Aircraft*
Alfred DePew, *The Melancholy of Departure*
Dennis Hathaway, *The Consequences of Desire*
Rita Ciresi, *Mother Rocket*
Dianne Nelson, *A Brief History of Male Nudes in America*
Christopher McIlroy, *All My Relations*
Alyce Miller, *The Nature of Longing*
Carol Lee Lorenzo, *Nervous Dancer*
C. M. Mayo, *Sky over El Nido*
Wendy Brenner, *Large Animals in Everyday Life*
Paul Rawlins, *No Lie Like Love*
Harvey Grossinger, *The Quarry*
Ha Jin, *Under the Red Flag*
Andy Plattner, *Winter Money*

Frank Soos, *Unified Field Theory*
Mary Clyde, *Survival Rates*
Hester Kaplan, *The Edge of Marriage*
Darrell Spencer, *CAUTION Men in Trees*
Robert Anderson, *Ice Age*
Bill Roorbach, *Big Bend*
Dana Johnson, *Break Any Woman Down*
Gina Ochsner, *The Necessary Grace to Fall*
Kellie Wells, *Compression Scars*
Eric Shade, *Eyesores*
Catherine Brady, *Curled in the Bed of Love*
Ed Allen, *Ate It Anyway*
Gary Fincke, *Sorry I Worried You*
Barbara Sutton, *The Send-Away Girl*
David Crouse, *Copy Cats*
Randy F. Nelson, *The Imaginary Lives of Mechanical Men*
Greg Downs, *Spit Baths*
Peter LaSalle, *Tell Borges If You See Him:*
    Tales of Contemporary Somnambulism
Anne Panning, *Super America*
Margot Singer, *The Pale of Settlement*
Andrew Porter, *The Theory of Light and Matter*
Peter Selgin, *Drowning Lessons*
Geoffrey Becker, *Black Elvis*
Lori Ostlund, *The Bigness of the World*
Linda LeGarde Grover, *The Dance Boots*
Jessica Treadway, *Please Come Back To Me*
Amina Gautier, *At-Risk*
Melinda Moustakis, *Bear Down, Bear North*
E. J. Levy, *Love, in Theory*
Hugh Sheehy, *The Invisibles*
Jacquelin Gorman, *The Viewing Room*
Tom Kealey, *Thieves I've Known*